ACCEPTANCE

ACCEPTANCE

A novel of terror and love

Myrta Willy

authorHOUSE®

AuthorHouse™
1663 Liberty Drive
Bloomington, IN 47403
www.authorhouse.com
Phone: 1-800-839-8640

First published by AuthorHouse   02/02/2012

ISBN: 978-1-4678-8423-5 (sc)
ISBN: 978-1-4678-8424-2 (ebk)

Printed in the United States of America

CONTENTS

Chapter 1 The Contact 1

Chapter 2 The Show 43

Chapter 3 The Acceptance 81

Chapter 1

THE CONTACT

It was just before nightfall when she found herself entering the dense garden for the first time. Today was a winter day and heavy with dampness and mist, where the flames of the lamps flickering through the foliage seemed to beckon like assembly points. This habit of hers to be there late in the afternoon began when her rambles in the dark green countryside became more frequent, becoming part of her daily routine. It began some time ago, she didn't know exactly when, but the changes of the seasons and the whispering of the trees that was heard according to the time of day or night was enough for her.

"Yeah, I'll bet trees whisper!" Kostas would have taunted her if they had not broken up what seems like eons ago. No, it was not that long ago, it was in fact just a few months before, but the relationship with that person seemed so far away. Fine, she would admit, trees do not whisper, but they do quiver in the wind, with the rain seeping into the leaves, as well as the darkness that weighs heavily against their bulk.

"Trees do not whisper and darkness does not disrupt," he would correct her and continue, "You are moonstruck". He would make her mad and that was why they broke up. But at that time, she did not yet know of the forest-sized garden situated along the borders of the city. Until recently, she had rambled aimlessly among the hills, faraway country-sides and coastlines, until she suddenly found herself inside this huge expanse.

How did this happen? She could not remember. It was as if a mist covered her memory, revealing only her long slender shadow wandering along the narrow pathways until she was stopped by a similar male shadow, a dark figure half slouched on a bench. The man had a flat, motionless face, similar to a photograph inside a picture-frame. This was her first thought, followed by a second that he was around her age . . . around twenty five. A sweet young man despite his harsh pale countenance.

"He must be sick," she reasoned and stopped in front of the bench to look at the young man's picture-like face.

"My appearance has nothing to do with sickness," he answered, as if he had heard her reasoning, and after uttering these words, his picture-like lips reverted to their motionless smile.

"In other words" she wondered, "What are you trying to say?"

"I am lost, all was in vain," he placed a final period to his statement, moving his lips imperceptibly while forming these words as his mouth reverted back again to its frozen expression. His smile was not sad or worried, but rather steady . . . so steady that it seemed that nothing could remove it. The face of a desperate person, a gloomy and depressive look that was consciously afraid, but she did not move away. In fact she was preparing to ask him why he was as he stated lost.

"My name is Stefanos," he said, and added his last name in the silence that followed, "Stefanos Stamoulis." He continued in a voice that was somewhat questioning, "What's your name?"

"Elvina," the young girl immediately replied, an unusual name that she liked.

This acquired name hid no mysteries, no noble heritage. The nobility always gave themselves fancy names that were subsequently inherited by their descendents, together with their estates. She was not however of noble birth, but her name was neither common nor usual. It sounded nice, silky as velvet as it contained soft consonants such as "l" and "n" and the simple vowels of "a", "e" and "i". She liked her name. It was given to her by an imaginative godmother who joined the names of her two grandmothers, "Eleni" and "Vasiliki", to name their granddaughter "Elvina". When she was a child, she would snuggle deep into her bed, her head hidden under the covers, and feeling warm and dark, she would transport herself to palaces made of velvet, lying half-naked and barefooted on the softness of silky curtains without stone walls and wooden floors.

She found herself wondering about this young man in the garden. What was he in fact trying to tell her?

"Why are you lost?" putting her puzzlement into words.

"Elvina!" he pronounced her name softly, fleetingly, as if trying to touch her. "If you come again, I will tell you," with his lips taking on that fixed bitter smile.

The young girl was about to insist on finding out when she suddenly felt alone, surrounded by multiplying shadows. The young man had disappeared, leaving her among rows of dark cypress trees and not within the softness of her childhood years. She shivered uncontrollably, feeling cold as if the sunless trunks of the trees chilled the warmth emanating from her body, but something kept her from leaving.

"I'll be back," she whispered and moved away with great effort. Kostas was right in calling her moonstruck. She blamed herself, believing that the shadows relaxing on the benches were talking to her as she moved down towards the gate.

It was the following day when her legs took her back there. She did not know how, whether by bus or by some other means or where she started from. She just found herself again walking up to the bench where she had met Stefanos. If Kostas was with her, she would prove to him that the trees whispered as she walked along the small narrow pathways.

"Did I lose my way?" she asked herself, but the narrow pathways were the same as before and the surrounding foliages—some fresh and flexible like green snakes and others half-dry—were still there, as were the statues and the ornate adornments scattered among them, but they lay in a diffused sort of silence that made them look all alike. How in fact did this silence cause this homomorphy? she asked herself without answering.

Then, in the ever so serene and quiet environment she heard the leaves sighing "That way", as if they were showing her the way by bending their branches, "Turn right!"

She looked around in case she recognized the path, since the day before she had not marked it. "I will never find it," she murmured. The young man would probably not return to the garden, even though he had asked her to meet him there.

"You've been like this all your life, don't give up now," a voice reached her ears from afar. It chased her away and she decided not to worry about the past as it was all over. She was determined to find the pathway, and this one led her to him.

"Good morning!" she articulated, feeling suddenly shy. What am I doing looking for a stranger in an unfamiliar place? This thought caused palpitations, making her want to run away before her legs froze and she remained with him.

"No!" she shouted. Some passersby looked at her in surprise but otherwise ignored her. Visitors to the garden were always quiet and reserved, so what was a shallow woman doing here, running around the pathways frantically looking for the exit, and was so frightened she kept coming back to where she started from . . . a true labyrinth.

She may have left but she was back the following day, sure of her destination. He would be there, waiting patiently for her while she shied away. She had always been timorous and frightened; she knew it and was forced to accept it at times.

She left home when she was fifteen, a home where having a double-barreled name laid heavily on the shoulders of a simple girl with few talents. After many attempts and hormone treatment over the years, her parents finally acquired her, pampering her when she was small, but went on to pressurize her to the full as she grew older, telling her how to cope with foreign languages, dancing and school.

"I am not suited for dancing," straightening her posture by stamping her foot, and they then sent her to the swimming pool. She never went there, it was that simple. She replaced her sports activities by spending all her time at the Internet café with the boys from her class or with other older boys, who muttered while looking at her furtively between the games and the sites.

"We will not kick you out if they don't want you at home" or "At least treat us to a coffee if you want to join us."

"I don't want to," she replied, sticking out her chin. This was followed by "Buzz off, you're breathing my air."

"How can you be breathing when you're already dead," she retorted.

"You're a jinx so push off, I won't say it again", they replied.

Stefanos was at least a strange case that attracted her immensely, despite her pensive glances at him. She could not remember if this event was new or old, if she had left and then returned to this spot or had she entered again as soon as she had reached the gate, but how could she turn her back on him. Fate must have played a strange game on this youth for him to be sitting alone on the bench.

"I've gone and lost him," she whispered to herself when she came across the empty bench, ready to blame herself for acting so thoughtlessly, as she would not see him again. Then she heard a quiet voice from behind her:

"Here I am," just barely announcing his presence. She turned around and saw him standing next to her, a young man with a picture-like face.

"Don't be afraid," he continued in the same quiet tone, calming her beating heart, and her reaction was that she felt his presence to be completely normal. She felt at ease when he said "Let's walk" and they began to stroll along the narrow pathways. They soon left the park and walked along the roads filled with vehicles and traffic.

"Speak louder, I cannot hear you!" Elvina could not hear him in all that noise.

"I had a car just like that one," he shouted into her ear as he pointed at a BMW sports car.

She looked at him doubtfully, as he did not fit the image of an expensive car owner. He did not have the necessary façade, nor was he well-dressed, but she never doubted his words.

"Why couldn't I have met you when you had that car," she said smiling feebly. His reciprocating smile did not resemble that of a still photograph, probably because her conversation raised his spirits, so he added in a teasing tone:

"You might have met me and I ignored you. Not that it was your fault, you are a great looking girl, but there are women aplenty." He then strutted around, straining his suit. Elvina did not reply, even though she did not like men to goad her since the Internet café period. She knew many lines such as "I eat kids with your attitude for breakfast" or simply "That's what they all say", but something kept her from uttering them.

It was during her Internet café fling that she decided to run away from home. She could not stand their criticisms: "Have you studied?" or "Why didn't you study?" or "They called from school that you did not go today" or "Your English teacher complained that you had not opened a book" or "Think about the money we are wasting on you."

The Internet café was therefore her security place where her girlfriend Natalia and she worked out their plan of action. They would collect money by continually asking for things from their parents. For example, they would say that their shoes had worn out, and would then buy cheap shoes instead of new expensive ones. They would pocket the money given to them for schoolbooks or gifts for their teachers, sucking it in like jellyfish. They even stooped to supposedly sending money to aid the children in Ethiopia.

And when they decided that they had collected enough money, they asked themselves, "Where can we now go?" This was a rhetorical question as there was only one answer—Athens! They arrived in the city one morning by sea, after telling their parents not to expect them home as they were leaving on a school-trip. They left the ship in Piraeus, which would probably be the first place their parents would look for them, and headed towards Glyfada.

After a week or so, they decided to save money so they acted accordingly and moved in with a bachelor, who later threw them out when they did not respond to his ulterior motives.

"Imagine him wanting to sleep with us," cursed Natalia. But it was now November and they had not planned for the cold weather as they were still wearing summer clothes. It was between bar-hopping, travelling back and forth by tram, trying out clothes all day at the shops but not buying any so as save their dwindling money and staying out late every night, that Elvina caught a bad cold.

"It's nothing, it'll pass," she told herself every morning as she forced herself to get out of bed. But on the fourth day she was burning with a fever and could not open her eyes or even to stand on her feet.

"What am I to do with you?" asked Natalia. "We are meeting the guys at twelve".

Elvina motioned her to go with her hand and then turned over. When Natalia returned late that afternoon, she found Elvina lying in bed unconscious, and began swearing at her friend.

"You decided to get sick now that we're having such a good time," she cursed, but their money was running out and this was a major problem. So she phoned for an ambulance and then contacted their parents.

The doctors treated her pneumonia just in time. "I don't even know how I managed to live" she contemplated as she walked along the crowded streets with Stefanos, quickly crossing at the corners as the cars stopped one behind the other, forming long lines as they waited.

"Hurry up! Walk faster as I want to pass that red car," she cheerfully shouted at her companion as she pointed at a stationary car.

"What do you expect with this traffic," he did not share her enthusiasm and began showing signs of melancholy. His face was expressionless with only his lips forming that well-known smile. His good mood had disappeared.

"I was going to change it" he grumbled, pointing to the car he had bragged he had. "I did not have the time to sell it. The gears were shot. My parents have probably sold it," he sighed.

"Tell me about yourself. You promised me," she reminded him.

"I can't in all this commotion. Let's go back," he snapped back at her and turned back without waiting for her.

Her family cared for her and did not scold her when she was sick. They helped her to recuperate, reminding her when she should take her antibiotics and her cough syrup, they gave her milk to drink to make her stronger, and they took her for her X-rays and blood tests. When her health was better, they dealt with her psychism.

"Why did you both leave? What didn't you like?" They addressed her in the plural form to include her co-accomplice. Elvina replied with four words:

"It was a fling" and put an end to this situation, leaving her with a sensitive respiratory system and an attitude change by her parents. No more lessons and swimming pools.

"If you don't feel well, don't go to school today" and "What can I cook for you today?" All previously banned activities were now proposed. "Don't tire yourself reading" and "Andreas, doesn't she look pale?" her mother worriedly asked her father, referring to her color. There were no more things that had to be done. Instead, it was now "What does my little girl want?" They preferred her to be strong and healthy and not sit her down for exams and university.

Elvina took full advantage of 'Whatever our little girl wanted'. She used the word "whatever" to encompass everything she could think of. She never opened a book, she skipped school whenever she felt like it, she bought whatever worthless item caught her eye, from hair clips to fake jewelry. Within a short period of time she had changed from a promising student to a spoilt brat. But a sweet spoilt brat at that because, even though her cheeks turned red only with the addition of rouge, she was changing into an attractive girl with a svelte figure. As for the face hidden by her hair, she transformed her paleness into sadness, giving herself an air of charm and mystiqueness.

She now however wanted to reach Stefanos who was ahead of her. They each in turn passed through the gate of the garden where, under the trees surrounded by an aura of silence, she stopped him by grabbing him by the elbow.

"Come let's sit down on the bench so you can tell me about yourself," she proposed. Elvina noticed that the bench was situated under a huge pine tree, opposite a small church from where chanting could be heard.

"I can't stand newcomers arriving here every day," murmured Stefanos. Elvina rationalized that he did not feel like opening up or perhaps he considered her to be one of them. But before she could ask him to explain what he meant, a man sat on the bench next to them. He looked over sixty, short and thin like a teenager, hyperkinetic and angry.

"Are you new?" he addressed Elvina, "Tell me, you ignoramus."

"Shut up!" imposed Stefanos.

"Okay!" the new arrival did not persist.

"I probably made a fool of myself," Elvina thought, paraphrasing his words, "since I am sitting on benches with strangers." At that moment some people came out of the little church and walked off in all directions.

"But you are however a knockout," admired the elderly-looking ugly teenager.

Stefanos introduced the stranger. "This is Nontas, an ambulance driver."

"I am leaving now," Elvina said as she stood up.

"Come back sometime," exhorted the driver, "We didn't have much time now, so we'll talk again next time".

"Be careful as he may win you over and once he starts you can't escape," replied Stefanos in a deriding tone. "We're also leaving," he added and they both headed towards the depths of the garden. Elvina watched in amazement as their departing figures blended into the foliage of the trees, and they soon disappeared from sight blending in with the passersby, causing her to tremble inexplicitly.

"She is as beautiful as an actress I met years ago," Nontas was at that same time expressing his thoughts to Stefanos. "We were called in by a theater. We arrived quickly and found that she had fainted. We threw some water on her and loosened her clothing. She did not respond, she was unconscious, passed out. We placed her in the ambulance where she remained unresponsive with her eyes closed."

"What happened with the audience? Did the performance stop?" wondered Stefanos.

"The woman was dying and all you can think of was the audience. Don't you care about her?"

"Why should I care about her? It wasn't as if I knew her."

"If I tell you her name, I'm sure you've seen her either at the theater or on television. She played in a serial that lasted for years; it was of course a minor role."

"Say I knew her. That doesn't change anything."

"I swear I've never met a more cold fish than you."

"I'm this cold because no one has ever cared about me, so why should I care about them. Anyway, forget about me, what happened to your actress friend?"

"For your information, the show was still in the rehearsal stage, so don't worry, the enjoyment of the show-loving audience was not affected. The little lassie was revived in the ambulance about a kilometer from the theater. I heard all this as I drove the ambulance. I don't know exactly what they did to her but she sat up smiling.

Her first words were, 'I'm not sick, leave me alone.'

'What do you mean lady? You caused such a commotion in the theater and with the Ambulance Department, and now you have nothing?'

'I was pretending,' she exclaimed proudly.

'You mean you didn't actually faint?' We all looked at her in amazement. She looked so fine, so lively and bursting with health."

"What happened then," asked Stefanos to show that he was interested, even though what he really wanted now was to get rid of Nontas and his loquaciousness?

"'I'm fine', she repeated triumphantly, 'Nothing was wrong with me. I fell down and remained motionless. I did not move a muscle, no matter what they did to me. I convinced everyone and I just laid back and listened to them running back and forth shouting 'What happened to her?' 'How can we help her?' 'She has no pulse,' 'She has no color, she's so pale.' 'I was always pale. Just before I pretended to have fainted, I went to the toilet and removed my make-up. Again, I'm fine', she repeated for the umpteenth time."

Nontas continued, "'The woman is fine, I added.' The paramedics all mocked me saying 'The expert has spoken.'

'Why did you do all this?' I asked her.

'I wanted to play a leading role,' she confessed, 'but who would give me the opportunity. I spent many hours waiting outside the offices of one or another producer to see me. But even if they did see me, good roles are few and far apart so who would play these leading roles? Who played in Ipsen, Tennessee Williams or Edward Alby?'

'Who are they,' interrupted one of the paramedics.

'Theatrical writers,' she confided, 'I have always dreamt of playing their works, but who has such luck . . . 'She did not complete her phrase, giving herself little chance of playing such roles.

Here Stefanos allowed a mocking smile to flitter across his face. Nontas ignored this and carried on.

"'You deserve them, you were perfect,' I congratulated her, taking my hands off the steering wheel to clap.

'Watch out! We'll crash!' shouted the paramedics.

'You really tricked us all, ain't that the truth, guys?' asking the others for confirmation as I again put my hands on the steering wheel.

'You sure did', confirmed one of the paramedics while the other continued suspiciously, 'I still don't believe that she is okay,' frightened that maybe she was sick and they would consequently find themselves in deep trouble.

I decided to take the initiative, 'Where do you stay, Miss? We'll take you home a winner. This may not be a limousine, but who cares.' We dropped her off a block from her home so that her neighbors would not see her and begin the questions."

"She really thought she was someone," said Stefanos, putting an end to the story.

Elvina had played various roles throughout her life, roles that were not actually roles but rather a way of life. She managed to finish high school by deceiving her teacher, "But I did study!" begging for him to understand her lack of studying. The Math teacher passed her by personally solving the questions in the test, concluding that "Elvina is not a numbers girl. Let her get her high school diploma and relieve the pressures on her."

Her father sent money to Athens so that she could rent an apartment, study computers and finish her English courses. Not a word about taking college entrance exams, which were now a thing of the past, following her running away from home and subsequently falling ill.

The money was not a lot, just enough for a small one-roomed apartment without a view, as her parents earned just enough to make ends meet, but they rationalized what could she do on the island. Let her spend a few years in Athens and then they would decide what to do.

Elvina spent the money for her language lessons on two huge pot plants, transforming her skylight into a real forest, showering more care on these plants than on herself. She watered them twice a week, added fertilizer and polished the leaves, and that was when she discovered that plants whispered. She would open the door and the tender branches would quiver in the wind, emitting sounds that seemed to say: "Elvina is sulking today."

"How can I not be in a sulking mood," she thought indignantly, "I spend all my time in front of a monitor and not a mirror, bored to tears. What do I care about folders and files, saving and deleting. One day I'll press a general 'delete' and who knows where you will all end up." She ended up caressing the leaves of her plants, letting them know that she did not mean all that she prattled to her greenery.

"Elvina is looking for something?" they wondered another time.

"I don't know what I'm looking for," she responded. "Where can I find it?" she pondered as she laughed with herself, coughing when the weather was humid.

She was however having a pretty good time. She spent the rest of her tuition money on a soft, silk settee cover, cuddling up on it for hours as she watched television.

"How can you spend so much time doing nothing?" asked her previous friend when he found her spread out on the comfortable settee.

"Easily," she replied in order to get rid of him. "Why should I tire myself studying lessons and then spending eight hours going back and forth to the office," she once confided.

"And how will you live?"

"I'm not living so badly, am I?" In fact, the money for her language lessons allowed her to buy some beautiful clothes, through which she met an older man.

"Fortyish," she was forced to confess to Natalia, who persisted, "Only! Tell me the truth!"

"I never saw his identity card," said Elvina sulking.

"Married?" her friend continued the interrogation.

"How should I know," replied Elvina vaguely. In fact, she never asked him as long as the affair lasted and he never told her. Nor did she want to know where he spent the hours and days he was not with her. When he called her and she was in the mood, they would go out and have a good time. In exchange, he spoilt her solid.

"The first thing was my name," confided Elvina to Stefanos as they sat on the bench.

"It's strange how you pronounce it as if you're kissing silk," he replied.

"Its individuality made me feel different," she confessed. "Don't forget, after my illness my parents gave me everything I wanted, they spoilt me and this boomeranged."

"No one spoilt me," exclaimed Stefanos.

"What about your sport cars and your girlfriends, as you told me the day before yesterday." This date was just an expression that no one contended as no one could say how much time had passed since their last meeting.

"We're talking about you now," he refused to open out about himself.

"Next was the man who was more than fifteen years older than me. He was called 'Mr. Big' by Natalia because she was insanely jealous. She went out with youngsters who made her pay for her coffee. My Mr. Big paid for everything, and besides I now had no money to spare as my father's work had fallen and it was only with great difficulty that he was able to send me pocket-money. Mr. Big . . ." Elvina remembered with nostalgia, "would disappear for days on end and then suddenly call me and come and pick me up. We would go on trips or just drive around until sunrise."

"Did you love him?"

"How should I know? Don't make things difficult for me," grumbled Elvina. "He would buy me clothes and jewelry, like this one I'm wearing around my neck. He also bought me a ring but I don't know where I put it, I must have misplaced it. We would eat at expensive restaurants, It was fantastic living!"

"You call this way of life fantastic, I think it sucks," replied Stefanos as he ignored her by turning his back on her.

She got really mad but before she could respond, a small boy, nine or ten, came running down the pathway and fell into her arms. His head was completely bald, not even one hair on it.

"Chemotherapy," he answered her wondering gaze in his childish voice, easily pronouncing this difficult sounding medical term. "Three times a month," he added as if in a bragging tone, "First the hospital and then dead on my feet. I can't even find my bed. I slept one day in my brother's room and he screeched like a cat as he thought I was contagious. He hasn't entered my room since.

"Will you bring me a ball when you come again?" asked the little boy in a demanding voice, without warning or in continuation to his last words, thus waking up Elvina from the grief caused by the flashback to his illness.

She now looked at the small boy and realized he seemed to be a happy boy with lots of uncut brown hair falling across his forehead and over his ears. Being bright, he saw her astonishment and went on to explain.

"It's been quite a while since I stopped chemotherapy," the word was like chewing gum as he used it much more than any other word, "so my hair grew again. According to my mom, I don't have nice hair. It's girlish as she strokes it. Will you bring me a ball? I'm fine and I can kick a ball, so buy me one so I can kick it over the fence." He ran towards the fence, tracing the route the ball would take until he disappeared into the trees, where some impish figures wandered around restlessly, competing with each other to see which one could hide first.

Elvina, concerned about the curious events that were taking place before her, syllogized that the garden was haunted. As for the boy's hair, she couldn't one moment see him bald and the next with long brown-blond hair, so she decided to turn around and walk away.

However, it was the small boy who other than making her feel emotional also provided her with a reason to leave immediately to buy him a ball. She would go to the store and ask for a soccer-ball suitable for a ten-year old boy and not a larger ball more suitable for professional players. She pushed herself to walk more quickly with happy skip-like steps, as if she was the little boy going to the shops to buy toys.

She soon reached the department store specializing in sports goods, and travelled down the escalator to the basement with the other shoppers, who stood patiently and motionless as they allowed 'electricity' to transport them.

"A child's ball," she addressed the salesman who ignored her as while serving a grandfather who had come down the escalator with her. While awaiting her turn, Elvina looked at the various types and sizes of balls on the display stands. Since the salesman was still ignoring her, she decided to try out the soccer balls. She placed a couple of balls on the floor and began kicking them up and down on the plastic floor. The second one seemed to have a better bounce.

"Is this ball suitable for a child?" she asked as she showed it to the salesman, as she was impatient to buy it quickly and return to the garden so that the small boy could play with it before nightfall. The indifferent salesman however did not even look at her, nor did he admonish her to replace the balls back onto the shelves. His full attention on a customer as he stated the advantages of the sports shoes the man wanted to buy. He finally disappeared behind a door to bring back various sized and styled shoes.

Elvina became very impatient as the customer tried out how comfortable each shoe was before the mirror. As she was preparing to catch the attention of the salesman, a youngster escaped from the attention of his mother who was still on the escalator and grabbed the salesman by the arm, asking for ski products. So mom, son and salesman moved to the back of the store to look at the products in question, with the salesman abandoning the shoes' customer and Elvina without a second thought.

Elvina sighed as they disappeared behind the display stands and sports equipment and replaced the balls back onto their stands. She was just preparing herself mentally to wait patiently when a whole team of screaming kids came striding down the escalator. There was no way the salesman would now spend any time with her, and anyway, it was getting dark outside. She rose up the escalator without moving a step, thinking what would the young boy now say?

"I couldn't buy him the soccer-ball," she announced to Stefanos who appeared before her at the entrance to the garden, which she had previously ignored for a long time as she had then wandered around the countryside outside the city.

The boy who had asked for a soccer-ball was nowhere in sight. This was the first time or probably one of the few times when Elvina would go into a shadowy park at dusk and she liked it, whether it was late afternoon with a mauve sundown or a twilight mist falling like a grey cloak . . . both suited her. She further discovered that at that specific time she did not often meet the boy with the bald head or with a head covered in hair.

"Forget him," advised Stefanos, "He's always asking for balls, not including the ones his mother bought for him. His mother is always buying him new things."

"Okay!" Elvina felt more tranquil now since she had really taken this affair to heart. She could not buy a simple ball, she who would go into a boutique and empty all the shelves with the money of Mr. Big, as he had been nicknamed by Natalia. This arose when she decided with Natalia to act all coquettishly with him and tell him sweetly, "Why waste your time looking for things to buy me and not just give me the money to buy what I really want?" This could not be interpreted as 'I want money to be with you' but rather 'Since you want to spend your money, let me utilize it."

He of course accepted this with alacrity, "You've lifted a load off my shoulders," and since then he had filled her bag with money that was more than enough to raise her living standards.

Natalia whistled admiringly as she opened the wardrobe. She ended up wearing most of the clothes herself, while at some stage Elvina began to resent this.

It would of course be a lie to say that she wasn't enthralled by the wonderful expensive clothes, especially the quality of the fabrics. She believed in quality, in contrast to other girls her own age whose only thoughts were clothes that were in fashion.

With the palm of her hand she caressed the cashmere sweaters lying on the shelves without unfolding them, while the salesgirls looked at her suspiciously in case she soiled them. The next phase was to feel the fabric on her bare skin. She tried everything that was in season but those she preferred were woolen and fleecy for winter and fine, thin clothes for summer. Silk drove her wild while velvet was her weakness since her name 'emitted a velvety sound'.

Natalia selected whatever suited her. "Why did you buy this," she complained about a velvet skirt, "It's ugly, I wouldn't wear it even if I was eighty."

Elvina defended her choice by taking it out of the cupboard and holding it next to her cheek, whispering "It can hear you, don't talk like that" as she caressed it.

"I think you're demented," scolded Natalia, as Elvina maintained a personal relationship with her clothes, as she did with her plants.

In contrast, her relationship with Mr. Big was waning, as if the fact that he gave her money instead of bringing gifts was at fault, and this seemed to placate them both. The fact was however that their meetings gradually tapered off randomly, limited only to enclosed areas; i.e. hotel rooms or inside a car.

"He's tired of me, I'm bored with him, it just can't go on," she confided to her friend and decided to accept it. She stopped going out with him, but there was something missing from her rationalized decision to break up with him. There was something else other than boredom.

One evening Elvina trembled with the need for some human contact, exactly like today when her feet dragged along the green-filled garden. So on that particular wet and cloudy evening, like now, she let him pull her under the sheets and undress her without speaking.

She loved his hands and his loving. Mr. Big was masculine and not much over forty, and when Elvina would let herself go and really enjoy him and not just pretend, she would melt with desire. So on that particular evening she was with him in the room, lying in his arms, and it was so good it scared her. This was then the reason why she broke off their relationship. What would she do when she fell in love with him and he subsequently left her?

This was why she played it absentminded and detached. One time he noticed this as they were eating in the semi-dark upper floor restaurant and Elvina was lost in the music. She dreamily moved her fork up and down to the beat of the music, pecking at her food as her ear and her attention were tuned in to the rock music.

"Where are you?" he asked as he shook her. She jumped in surprise.

"Where am I? I'm here right opposite you," she gathered herself as she went onto the offensive and madness.

"Whatever," he did not continue as their relationship did not include asking questions beyond that of "What time do we meet and where?" or "What do you prefer, sea or mountain?"

""You've been going out so long and you don't know if he's married or not?" queried Natalia.

"What do I care?" Elvina replied indifferently, "We're together as long as we're having a good time. That's all."

"I could never do that," snorted Natalia, "not knowing anything about him."

"Of course I do!" replied Elvina, "He's making a ton of money that he likes to spend."

"Doesn't he ask you how you spend your time?"

"I reply that I sleep a lot."

"That's true!" replied her girlfriend, putting an end to their conversation as it was leading nowhere.

One night after their lovemaking, he asked her if she liked it.

"Oh yes, very much!" She assured him and it was true but she was so tired and all she wanted to do now was to sleep quietly and dream.

When she replaced him with a student, they would talk to each other ten times a day, every day. He would call her on his cell-phone and give her a complete rundown of where he was at that time, where he was going, what he was going to do until their next conversation, and where he would be for the next ten years: post-graduate studies, work, career, etc, while Elvina would rarely speak about herself.

There was the classic "I'm at home," followed by "At the shops" and sometimes "At college." Her lies soon followed: "I'm at an interview for a role" or "I'll be on television."

He would ecstatically treat her to ice cream while Elvina paid for hamburgers. They would kiss between their Cokes and melted cheese while thinking about future glories. She left him when she got tired of inventing fictitious stories and unfulfilled achievements.

With Mr. Big she didn't have to talk, he spoke for both of them, narrating past and planning future trips, describing places without caring if she was listening to him or not. She would cuddle up next to him, opening her eyes widely when the car would stop, saying "Have we arrived already?" and he would laugh. She allowed his words to lull her to sleep, since she was afraid of being awake next to him. What would she do if she grew more attached to him and became indispensible.

When he began to limit their relationship, Elvina broke up immediately as she was now ready. This was the real reason why she left him, she was able to leave him before his loss became unbearable, but this she hid from both her friend as well as from herself.

Her second but more serious omission was her cough. She pretended she did not have it and she pretended she did not hear it. In a moment of truth, she wondered where this would lead her but subsequently banished it from her mind as she looked for Stefanos.

After reassuring her as to the young boy and the ball she did not buy, he turned away and walked deeply into the dense vegetation where only a narrow pathway separated the rows of trees, together with the falling dusk that darkened the atmosphere.

"Where are we going?" she managed to utter in a quivering voice while other figures passed by them at the crossing, some glancing at them while others just ignored them. As they were strolling along the pathway, a man passed by them without showing any interest in them as he was engrossed in his peculiar strides, supported on two deformed legs with defective soles that had not developed normally, even though the rest of his body was normal. They looked like appendages that had not been used, the legs of a cripple who dragged them along laboriously as he moved along the pathway.

"Look!" Elvina drew his attention to this strange figure that continued to move along, "Look!" she repeated as she couldn't believe what she was seeing.

"It's the cripple," explained Stefanos, "He was born like that and has spent all his life in a wheelchair. Since coming here, he hasn't stopped walking; he walks from morning to night.

"Let's leave, I'm scared!" she exclaimed as she dragged Stefanos by the sleeve. "Let's leave, I don't understand anything, I don't know what's happening to me," she continued as she trembled in fright.

"He's disappeared from sight," he replied as a mocking smile began to form on his lips.

Elvina was certain that strange things were happening around her, things that she was witnessing. "Where are you taking me?"

"Follow me," replied the man without looking at her as he continued to walk on.

Elvina had no choice but to follow him. If she turned back she would surely lose herself deeper into the labyrinth of dense vegetation. Even the light was against her, deserting her in giant leaps, so she carried on, scared out of her wits, until she reached the tall thick wall that separated the serene green expanse from the noisy cement world.

At the corner she came across a pavilion with steel rails that held up the climbing creepers. As she drew closer, she could discern the thin steel rails that supported the foliages, and there was also a dome-like roof made of the same material. Stefanos disappeared through an opening and lay down on the ground covered with sprouting grass and wild flowers.

"What is this place?" Elvina managed to croak, her tremors now apparent.

"A little house in a garden," replied Stefanos to satisfy her curiosity. "Two eccentric people made it."

"Do you know them?" she asked in a trembling voice.

"They were a couple that really loved each other," responded Stefanos. "They spent a lifetime together, over fifty years."

"Do you know them? She asked again.

"He was a tall aristocratic gentleman with his wife."

"Where are they now? Elvina asked curiously.

"Do you want to meet them?" his voice was flat and neutral. "They don't go out very often," he continued in the same quiet voice. "I come here to be alone," he changed the subject by describing the surrounding vine-filled area that looked like a fairy-tale house in the darkness.

"You said they loved each other?" The aura emitted by the pavilion was gradually affecting Elvina, soothing her and allowing her at the same time to enjoy the sensation of two people in love with each other. This was not something that occurred very often.

"A great love story," she heard his voice sounding nostalgically without giving more details. He then left her to imagine the two figures wearing clothes dating back to the 1920s and 1930s—long skirt, top hat and umbrella—as they strolled under the trees.

"Something like that," the young man smiled and for the first time his smile was not a motionless picture-like smile but rather a live smile that was able to leave his lips.

"We must come back here again," proposed Elvina as she had discovered through her beating heart a place that touched her and made her want to love it.

This is what she should have done with the man who was older than herself, she should have let herself fall in love with him for as long as it lasted and not detach herself from him, and worst of all, she demeaned their relationship by asking for money instead of gifts.

Yes, this was despicable, this capped their rapport, together with her refusal to let herself feel anything. She now realized this in the pavilion, which together with the dense vegetation, brimmed over with tenderness and romanticism. Who knows where the woman who created all this is now, thought Elvina, wanting to meet her but afraid at the same time.

She was exhausted as she sat down on the grass next to Stefanos, and discovered that being under the foliage smothered her with greenery as well as silence.

"Silence is nice," she decided to speak out and tell Stefanos a story, hoping to shatter this silence with her voice, even as it exalted her.

There were a group of us in a bar. It was small, the decibels of the music flowing out of the loudspeakers were normal, we could talk to each other, but the bar however was filled with people. The person standing next to me did not stop talking, his bass-toned voice insisting 'I want that opening. I am going to get that job.' There was an opening in his company and he wanted the promotion. 'They must give it to you!!' screamed his girlfriend, 'You deserve it. You kill yourself working from morning to night.'

'If I had money, I wouldn't do anything, I would take it easy all day and let the others kill themselves working,' sighed the man to my left. I listened until I was dizzy in the head and suddenly screamed out aloud, 'You're strangling me with 'I want . . . ', 'If I had money . . . '. Shut up and let us listen to some music.'

But they couldn't keep their mouths closed for more than a minute, time enough for them to regroup and curse me, while at the same time pandemonium reigned in the bar." Elvina started laughing, hoping to justify herself. We're all in the same boat she rationalized, so why should she treat Mr. Big any better, or all those others and finally all those who were to follow.

But Stefanos was elsewhere and the only thing he heard from all that she had uttered was the word 'music', and this in conjunction with the magic of the pavilion, sparked his smile and his desires.

"Let's go to a bar," he proposed slowly. "I've missed it, let me take you there. It's flashier than yours was, it's a trendy place so it's crowded every day." As he was talking to her about the bar, it was if he was initiating her to it, and she found herself glued to him among many men and women, smoke and aromas. Her eyes were irritated but there was no space for her to raise her hand to rub them.

"It's hell but I love it," she whistled into his ear by standing on her toes as he pushed his way through the crowd. Being more agile than the others, he managed to work his way through, pulling her behind him as they moves into a corner. They were standing of course but were isolated from the hordes and so they could stand back and watch the commotion unrolling before them.

"This is where I met her," he found the moment to confess. Elvina looked around her, she had not been here before but it seemed to be in style with a great looking crowd. "She crushed her body onto mine, as we did earlier, and I glued my mouth to her ear to introduce myself.

'Stefanos,' I told her. 'Since we were pushed together, let's exchange names.'

'You think so,' she scolded me but her eyes were smiling.

'And telephone numbers,' I continued on relentlessly.

'You like to suffer,' she admonished him, 'but if you were wearing my high heels and if they had trod on your toes at least three times, I'll tell you how you'd be feeling.' But it was a start that she was talking to me.

'What about leaving?" I proposed.

'We could leave but my friends are around somewhere,' she replied.

'Let's go and you can send them a message that you've met the man of your dreams,' and I nibbled her ear and the ends of her hair with my lips as I said whatever came to mind. She couldn't misunderstand me as we standing so close to each other."

"As we were before," confirmed Elvina.

"Even closer together," said Stefanos reminiscently, "I pulled her towards the exit. It proved quite easy to leave and we were soon sitting on the comfortable seats of a nearby cafeteria. She finally sighed and took off her shoes. We were comfortable and easy-going with each other from the first moment, her name was Mara."

"That doesn't mean anything," commented Elvina, who was feeling somewhat jealous. In any event, has anyone spoken about me in this manner? she wondered. "How some women manage to hook their man and make him crawl at their feet just by taking off their shoes," she finished caustically, but Stefanos did not hear a word, he was enthralled in the tenderness of the moments he was describing.

"We exchanged telephone numbers that night and then said goodnight. She returned to find her friends while I stood at the corner under a lamppost and sent a message to her cell-phone, I can't remember what I wrote," he looked enquiringly at Elvina. "I don't remember, why can't I remember?" and before you know it, a mask of sorrow and anger covered his face, from his forehead to his jawbone.

Why did he have difficulty in conveying grimaces and expressions in general? wondered Elvina, feeling a sliver of fear among so many people and noise. The bar overfilled with the young and music, including smoke that made her cough.

"I can't breathe, let's go," she told the sad-looking mask as soon as she was able to articulate a word in-between her coughing.

"Loosen up." The young man raised his hand to caress her hair. "You're okay now, you don't have anything," he assured her and Elvina immediately overcame her feelings of drowning that had encompassed her and began to gaze around her as she forget her sudden indisposition.

"What are you looking for and worrying so much? It was probably just a text message to her cell-phone, such as 'Good night' or 'Think about me' or 'I'll be thinking of you until we meet again'—something like that."

"I don't know, maybe," he pondered. "Anyway, it was good because the next day when I called her to get together, she accepted," and the harsh mask that covered his face softened somewhat. It seemed that he was still the stiff young man as they wandered around the pathways towards the exit. Did we leave earlier, pondered Elvina, or did I imagine the whole bar scene as he was speaking to me?

The lights that were now on lit up the route they were following. They walked among the weak illuminations that emitted a small circle around each lamp-post, but they were many and stretched on forever. The more they walked, the more the illuminating lights multiplied, they never seemed so many to her before, stretching over such a long distance.

I'll never come back here at night, she sighed as she quickened her pace to leave Stefanos behind and leave that place as soon as possible.

How did Stefanos, so young, end up so disillusioned, she asked herself, wondering whether he managed to go steady with the girl in the bar? Did they form a relationship? She had many questions to ask him as soon as they met again, even if she had to listen to the great love-affairs of his life since she herself had not experienced anything like this, both as a notion or as emotions.

When she was with Mr. Big, she pushed this away but now she wanted it. All I want is love, she wanted to scream as she walked along the cars and the traffic. Do you have any love to give me, a love like that of the couple who had built the pavilion, like that which her newly-found friend was describing?

Somewhere, sometime I will find it, she consoled herself. But her life had gone downhill since she had broken up with the man who was older than her, even her pot plants had turned yellow. However, her main problem was a lack of money. It was not that she had lost Mr. Big's money which she had in any event spent here and there, it was her father who was almost bankrupt and who echoed, "You have finished your studies, come back to the island. What are you doing in Athens?"

"Various things," she responded.

"Like what," he asked curiously.

"I attended a seminar on candle-making," she replied in an attempt to satisfy him, but this instead drove him mad. "Just think how great you feel when you form something out of molten wax around the string core," she continued with this conversation stopper.

The result was a compromise. Elvina would stay in Athens and look for a job while her father would try and send her whatever he could spare. In the past they had spoilt her and given her whatever their little girl wanted, now it was the opposite.

But she would never return to the island. "I promised myself," she confessed to Natalia.

"Big deal," teased her friend. "What will you do when the money runs out?"

"Not theirs," was the reply, as Elvina rose from the couch to pluck at the yellowed leaf of the nearby plant.

"Look for a job," her friend suggested, "or alternatively, someone rich."

She initially found a job as a salesclerk in a department store. But after two days standing eight hours a day behind the counter, with customers sometimes not in sight and other times forming a line giving her vertigo as to whom to serve first: "I want a size larger" or "This color does not suit me" or some other foolishness, she spent the third day in bed, continuing her morning sleep and her previous life.

In a great moment of inspiration, she turned to her mother, who sent her some money which just took off the problem for several months.

It was then that she met the student with the 'I want' and 'I will' of his bright future while she led him on with scenarios for television roles, since she had used her mother's money to attend acting classes. Finding both acting school and the fairytale boring, she left the student and never returned to the school, situated in a basement with a torn carpet that caused her both coughing and flushing spells; coughing because she was allergic and flushing because her heart beat faster and she flubbed her lines when asked to present her scene. What was she doing there?

"Whatever happened to that little actress who played dead?" she asked the ambulance driver who suddenly appeared in front of her like a bantam-sized stretched-out clown, with the expression of an imp ready for mischief.

"Why the long face, Elvina?"

"I remembered something," she replied vaguely.

"How should I know," he was just as vague in offering information. "I never saw her on television and as for the theatre, I've never stepped inside one. What can I say, it's very difficult today to succeed."

"I also tried to become an actress, but it didn't work out," confessed Elvina.

"Did I hear someone talking about my profession," a deep cultured voice was heard from somewhere, possibly from behind her. Elvina turned around and saw a thin, lean silhouette wearing a long, clinging dress that seemed to be balancing on tall sandals among the flowerbeds until it settled near the trunk of a tree opposite her.

"She's new," informed the ambulance driver.

"You're Marilena Evangelou," said the young girl in an amazed tone.

"You'll find many famous people strolling around this place," flaunted Nontas, while Elvina blushed in front of the theatrical diva, noticing that the woman could not take her eyes off her.

"My God! You look just like me when I was young," exclaimed Marilena as she stood motionless, her face expressing amazement. "Please move around," she addressed Elvina in the same authoritative tone, who subsequently moved around like a zombie. "You're undoubtedly the splitting image of me in my youth," the actress repeated conclusively and approached closer to examine the young girl. "Same characteristics, an airy body, you even have my hair, my wonderful hair . . .," the theatrical diva admired her, a strange elation following her initial surprise.

"Do I really look like you?" said Elvina disbelievingly. She had seen photos of Marilena Evangelou but they showed her at a mature age and she therefore could not understand how she resembled the diva.

"I've seen photographs of you in the theater that was named after you and I recognized you from them," Elvina's voice trembled with admiration, "but I never imagined that we looked alike . . ." The diva cut her off, continuing in a warbling and delightful voice:

"Of course, the theater that bears my name. I go there sometimes to find out what's happening in the theatrical world, and I of course help young aspiring actresses. A little while ago there was a young girl who recited her lines as if she was in a school play. I thought for a moment that I should go and show her how to act her role but I immediately thought of a better way to help her. That night when she was sleeping I enacted her complete role as she slept, and the following day she was wonderful. Even I was impressed as the producer congratulated her enthusiastically.

It does not suit me to have the theatre that bears my name presenting bad theatrical productions, so I try to oversee as much as possible. Do you want me to give you some lessons so you can make your life more beautiful?" She addressed her final remarks to Elvina, hoping to entice her.

"No!" replied the young girl in a panic-stricken voice. The actress was a legend, a star while she herself had no talent and everyone would see this. "I don't have what it takes," she admitted.

"So why then did you sign up at the school?"

"I'm trying to find what I want to do," confessed Elvina, "but I do know how to make candles. I made Christmas decorations that weren't so bad," she spoke modestly in front of the famous actress. "I sold three that were placed in shop windows, the others remained unsold. But the three I sold were displayed in the windows of the shops. I passed by them every day during the Christmas season to look at them. I made no money from them. In fact I did not even cover the costs to make them as I sold only a few."

Elvina stopped talking because it seemed that the diva was not following her chattering, she seemed more interested in those passing by them.

"I know him," she muttered to herself. "He was chasing me for months; jewelry, roses, little notes were coming and going from my dressing room. We did not have such a bad time," she concluded as she looked at the young girl conspiratorially. The ambulance driver had disappeared some time ago.

"Teach me how to love," Elvina asked the star impulsively, "instead of acting lessons." Hearing this, Marilena Evangelou's eyes suddenly flooded with tears and she disappeared from sight.

"What did you say to her?" Nontas thundered at Elvina as he suddenly appeared before her. "You've lost her now. You'll never see her again. That word exists only in her roles and not in her heart," he concluded as he looked at her grouchily.

Kostas was the one who helped Elvina to rally again after failing at work and at school. "Why are you wondering around like a zombie? Don't you have anything better to do with your life?"

They had met in Kifissia where Elvina had lost herself after wandering around aimlessly along the narrow shady roads. During that phase of her life she had begun her aimless rambles which later had led her to the greenery-filled park that she had ignored until then, both unnatural for a woman of her age.

Which twenty-two year old woman rides the buses continuously and ends up hours later in Kifissia or Varkiza? She'd get off the bus and stroll along the narrow streets or lie down on the sandy beach next to the sea for hours on end.

Whenever she felt hungry she would look for a nearby bakery and at dusk she would hang around the bus-stop to return back home. She was always changing her destinations and whenever she ran into traffic, she'd just get off the bus and gawk at the unknown neighborhoods, but she preferred the countryside and the seaside. It was a day like today where she could not find her way back to the bus-stop to return home, so she waved at the first car she finally saw, as she had not encountered another soul along the remote areas she was roaming, and asked the driver, "Could you please tell me how to get to the main road?"

"Walking?" was the first observation to her query.

""Yes!" she replied monolectically, as she did not resort to one of her many lies such as 'My car broke down' or 'My boyfriend left me here' or 'I ran away from home' as an excuse to the reason she was alone in the area.

"You're far away," and even now the man did not bother to inform her further.

"I like to walk, in which direction should I go?" This was as specific as a question could be.

"Jump in, I'll take you. It's getting dark and there's no one around. You'll just lose yourself."

"I don't just jump into the car of a perfect stranger," the young girl responded and carried on walking.

"Let me introduce myself then," the young man proposed as he parked along the side of the road and began to walk with her.

His name was Kostas and he lived near the main square. He worked in his father's bookstore and was preparing to open a second store in Pallini, which was an up-and-coming suburb.

"Why couldn't you own a bakery?" was her only comment as he narrated his life. She was hungry as she had not eaten since that morning and the walk in the clean air had just made her hungrier.

"There's a bakery near our bookstore," responded the bookstore owner.

"Let's go past there so I can get something to eat," requested Elvina.

Kostas took her to a cafeteria instead of the bakery, where they ordered toasted cheese sandwiches and coffee. Elvina listened to him as she ate, while he continued to treat her as he had her attention.

"Do you want another coffee, a pastry, they serve fantastic syrupy sweets and pastries here?" he offered, sweetening her with custard-filled pastries and flattery.

Elvina sat back to digest what she had eaten while inspecting him more carefully. She guessed that he must be five-six years older than she and had quite a few more centuries of wisdom. "What kind of books do you sell?" she asked just for the sake of asking.

"Everything!" he replied with gusto and pride.

"Even for someone like me who doesn't read?" challenged Elvina.

"Sure!" the man replied without choking up and continued, "You don't read as you say, but you walk in the countryside so you're not a lost cause."

When they were better acquainted, he asked her why she wandered around as if lost.

"You were interested in other things at the cafeteria," she retorted.

"That was just to raise your spirits, you were trembling so much from hunger and fatigue," he explained. Why do you still wander around remote areas?"

"I don't know. I just like it."

"This is not normal behavior," he tried to perk her up, but Elvina's situation was getting worse and worse. The money sent to her barely covered rent and food, so she stopped whatever she had started—computer school, language lessons and acting classes. Finally her job at the department store. But without a job how could she make ends meet?

She then began looking for another job. She bought lots of newspapers to look through the classified ads and closed some job interviews but never showed up. She rarely went out with her friend Natalia or her friends in general, and as for the student, she had left him a month ago.

"Let's live together," proposed Kostas, so as not to waste his time travelling back and forth to the centre to meet her. "Move in with me."

He did not have to try hard to persuade her as Elvina thought about the money that she would save and thus acted immediately. She moved in with him, couch and all, leaving behind her withered pot plants. Kostas soon found her a job working in the main square as a cashier at a supermarket. She was hired immediately as their neighbor recommended her.

When the bookstore had no customers, the young man would pass by the supermarket to see Elvina and she would give him bubble gum which he would put into a vase in his office. She would then take them and chew them.

"Why don't you buy your own gum from the supermarket?" he once asked her.

"Because these have passed through your hands," she responded.

"So what!" he insisted.

"They have your sweetness," she replied, and so he kissed on her mouth that was opening and closing as she chewed her gum.

"I used to take the bubble gum from the supermarket and give them to him," she narrated to Stefanos, happy about the goings-on that periodically came to mind. The green-rich vegetation and the foliages of the pavilion revoked these memories as the two of them sat there whenever they wanted to get away from other people. But the words 'bubble-gum' seemed mocking and this was expressed on the impassive face of Stefanos.

"How old were you then?" he asked her.

"This was a year ago but it seems that these memories come from afar."

"Not even fourteen-year olds act like this," he concluded, closing the subject. Elvina was not offended since the image of her unwrapping bubble gum in front of the bookcases was one of the few moments of magic that rarely takes place.

"Have you ever heard jazz?" Stefanos now asked her nostalgically, the question barely hanging in the air. He was not interested in whether Elvina had ever heard jazz or not, it was about him and Mara listening to it when they had met. "Have you been to Prague?" The young girl was more jealous of the city and less of its music.

"The city has the greatest jazz-players," explained Stefanos as he continued, "We went there to celebrate our one month relationship. This was the surprise I sprang on her," his expression now withdrawn and remote.

"I've never been to Prague, I've never been out of Greece. How far can you travel by bus? I managed to reach Lavrio but I don't care. Someday I'll go," she murmured.

"Close your eyes and let me take you there," proposed Stefanos imperatively, as if daring her to object. So she leaned onto the foliage on the rails and closed her eyes.

"We're in the main square where the clock is," she heard Stefanos' voice and it seemed that she herself was acting in the movie, as she saw herself walking with him through the city that she had never visited, with its palaces and famous bridge.

Her guide narrated that he had bought tickets for himself and Mara without telling her anything. And he also found a hotel and reserved a table at the jazz-bar, one of the most renowned in the city. "I don't know what was happening to me, Mara made me feel like a god, I felt I could do anything, nothing and nobody could stop me. When I was not with her, I would think of nothing else but her all the time . . . where was she now, what was she doing, was she thinking of me?"

"I would call her, asking what time was it.

'Don't you have a watch,' she scolded me fondly.

'I want to hear it from your lips,' I insisted.

'Three hours and twenty minutes remain before we meet again."

'Can't we make it twenty minutes,' I begged her.

'I can't make it, I just arrived home,' she replied stressed out. 'Let me catch my breath, take a bath and dress.'

'So let me come and watch you,' I begged her.

'Not today,' she replied, 'I look a mess.'

'I want to see you looking a mess.' I didn't back down as I missed her, I wanted to be with her all the time.

'Okay,' she finally gave in. 'Come at eight thirty instead of nine.'

This half hour that I gained meant a lot to me. The day we were to travel I didn't tell her anything. I just drove to the airport and parked in the parking area.

'Where are we going?' she enquired.

'Prague,' I replied as if it was the most natural thing in the world, just around the corner.

'I don't believe it,' she said and was then speechless.

'It's for our anniversary,' I reminded her.

'I don't have anything with me,' she said as she looked down at her body. She was wearing jeans and a sweater. I can see her in my mind, tall like you and incredibly beautiful as she looked at me as I pulled the tickets out of my pocket.

'Let's check in.' I put my arm around her waist and almost carried her until she recovered from her surprise. 'You can buy what you need from there,' I continued, overcoming her last resistance that she had no clothes to wear.

In the plane I gazed at her continuously, wanting to go into the cockpit and put the plane into orbit around the Earth, to circle it forever, when we finally landed.

'We're going to a jazz-bar,' I told her that first night.

'I haven't heard much jazz,' Mara confessed, 'but now I want to listen to it.'"

"It's really erotic music," Stefanos extolled jazz as he and Elvina passed through the door and the first husky notes reached her ears.

These were no silky melodies, these were notes emanating from instruments with difficulty, notes rendered with anguish and pathos by a soul dying of love. Elvina paused self-consciously, the music making her wonder where she was, with whom and why. She just wanted a man to fill her with kisses and promises, and she shivered as she wondered if Stefanos would ever do this.

"That's how Mara stood, just as you are now," she heard Stefanos' voice as if from afar. "I pulled her by the arm and led her to our table. Come with me Elvina," he pulled her and they sat deep in the bar. "It's the same table," he whispered, "You're sitting in her chair. She was wearing a long dress open at the back which I had bought her that morning. We sat opposite each other and just looked without speaking for quite some time, I don't know for how long. The maitre'd must have passed by our table at least ten times but we were enthralled by the music, so he did not bother us. He later left two glasses on the table and we drank to the rhythm of the music. I don't remember what we drank, it could have been water or nectar, I just don't know what he brought us. He finally asked us if we were ready to order.

"The woman devastated me," he finished suddenly as he unexpectedly completed his reminiscencing with intense emotions. Elvina, carried away by the music, placed her hand on his shoulder as the orchestra continued to play excruciatingly, the notes now seemed to scratch her flesh.

"I like jazz," she confessed to Stefanos.

"Mara also liked it," he replied in a chilling tone. His face was now devoid of any emotions as he looked apathetically at the people around him and the decor that was famous for its elegance and luxury. Elvina looked around her now that she was free of the captivating music. Men and women—elegant, tall and slender, as if the short, ugly and fat had been eradicated from the city centre.

They drank from crystal glasses and ate small portions from huge porcelain plates, they talked and they laughed, sometimes awkwardly but always relaxed and refined. "Where am I," she asked herself, while she could not imagine how she arrived there.

"Let's go!" Stefanos said unexpectedly. Even though she wanted to stay awhile, Elvina did not react. They walked out into a fine drizzle that did not wet them, as it seemed they were waterproof. The young girl allowed herself to walk next to him, but he was 'holding' his thoughts and not her hand.

Besides, she sighed, he was a stranger she had met sitting on a bench as he wept over his fate. And for a moment she wanted to walk away from him, but when she opened her eyes, she found herself standing opposite him in the pavilion, inside its shady and idyllic interior. She was certain they had not moved an inch, so how did he manage to deceive her so that she thought she was miles away. Maybe this was the reason why she came more and more often and not leave him for an instant . . . him and the shady park.

"Let's go outside," she wanted to get away from their closeness and from the erotic music that still aroused her. As they left, they bumped into the ambulance driver, as if this had been arranged. Elvina, not knowing what to say as she still had the jazz music on her mind, felt she had to express this feeling:

"I have just heard the most beautiful music in the world!"

"The music of course!" the short, lanky man opened his huge mouth. "It's something wonderful, grandiose. I must say that this music also attracts me, especially when I'm downing a glass of tsipouro and getting into the mood. One time we received an emergency call to hurry up and pick up a patient who had lost consciousness and had fallen down, hitting his head in the process. I gassed the ambulance while the siren wailed loudly, speeding and weaving through the traffic. And if one of those smart alecks tried to follow my ambulance and I had no patient inside, I would suddenly stamp on the brake and watch him spinning trying to avoid me."

"You're a real jerk," commented Stefanos dryly, who did not seem to have followed his conversation.

"Aren't I good enough for you," said Nontas in an offended voice.

"Forget him! Don't pay any attention!" Elvina gestured behind the back of the young man. "Tell us what happened!" not that she was really interested to hear his story, but he had helped her escape from the awkward moment of being alone with Stefanos, a stranger whom she was slowly falling in love with.

"Anyway, we reached the given address where we found the patient's daughter waving her hand at us to draw our attention. We placed him on the gurney, blood pouring from his head, unconscious from the head injury or from some other fateful episode. After so many years of experience I usually knew what they were suffering from, but this event stumped me.

Around the middle of the journey and with the pedal floored, the patient woke up and began whining.

'What's going on?' I asked the paramedic.

'He wants some music,' he replied indifferently as the whining continued on. Where would I find music in an ambulance. My colleague tried to calm him down as I turned the radio up loud so that they could hear me from behind and searched for some songs.

The paramedic passed on the preferences of the patient. I finally lowered the siren's volume and continued searching the radio stations.

'What are you doing?' asked my colleague, bringing me to my senses, 'Our job is to take him to the hospital and not provide him with music.'

The injured person continued to moan. 'Wait a moment," I said while still continuing my station hopping. As I quickly passed by the Third Program with its classical music, the patient shouted in jubilation, 'Here! Leave it here!'

I did not want to disappoint him so I left it there and just increased the volume to the full. The ambulance filled with musical instruments and melodious music. I'll never forget it as it was really something. I thought of increasing speed but I was enthralled with the symphonies that sometimes flowed like water in a creek and sometimes thundered like cannons, and before the three of us had realized it, we reached the hospital.

The security guard raised the bar when he heard my honking and I closed the radio as we drove in. 'Why! Don't close it!' I heard the patient complaining.

'We've arrived and the doctors will now look after you', I tried to raise his spirits. 'I'm going to die,' he replied, 'but at least I managed to hear the Ninth Symphony one more time and it was a hell of a rendition,' he continued talking as they rolled him into the building. The paramedic told me that he learnt that the patient was a musician when he was handed over to the doctors." And Nontas' voice slowly died down, indicating that he had nothing more to say.

"Did they save him?" Did he live?" said Elvina expressing her concernment.

"Do you think we ask about every patient we bring in? How do I know, my girl, we don't retain names, nor a register." Despite his indifference and harsh words, his voice was low-keyed. "The strange thing is . . ." he continued more loudly, "I tried listening to the classical music of the musician, but nothing doing. I just couldn't stand it so I changed the music. Where was that triumphant atmosphere that changed the ambulance into a church! I listened again and again to the Third Program, listening to various pieces but nothing stirred me."

"This type of music is not for your tastes," expressed Stefanos quietly but condescendingly, his voice just reaching Elvina's ears, while the ambulance driver turned around and disappeared.

"It's getting late, it's time for me to leave," said Elvina, overwhelmed by all that had occurred.

With her supermarket job securing her bubble-gum in addition to a salary, and her living with Kostas, which meant he paid the rent, her finances began to look good again. Elvina also had the money her parents still sent her as she did not tell them she was living with someone.

She never had a land phone so they always called her on her cell-phone. They couldn't 'see' where she was when they called her, while they stopped coming to visit her in Athens because she would not return back to the island.

Elvina was on a high roll for the next six months or so. Even her cough was reduced from chronic to isolated instances, as if her ramblings around the countryside were good for her health. And of course there were the games she was consciously playing, the first was the bubble-gum and the second playing Kostas' girlfriend who was living with her boyfriend.

He played being chef while she washed the pots or immersed herself in recipes she read in a cookbook she had discovered in his bookstore, and Kostas would try out everything she concocted.

They would run into each other in the bathroom but in general they managed until one day, Elvina woke up and found it impossible to wear the supermarket's uniform. It was summer and she wore it without anything underneath it, until one day the abrasive coarse material of the uniform repulsed her. She would never again allow her soft skin to come into contact with it, even though she had worn it continuously during the hot summer days.

She would of course not discuss this with Kostas. How could he understand that maybe the job was at fault and not the uniform? She who had slept between her velvety name and her dreams now she was reduced to wearing an old rag sitting behind a cash register, with her legs hanging, tapping in various goods, from ice cream and yoghurts to onions and cheeses, while she herself craved something more than the daily grind.

She pretended she was suffering from a migraine and spent the day running from the shower to the bed. The next day she was still feeling under the weather, but as soon as Kostas left for the bookstore, she ran out the next moment. Not for the woods but rather the city centre which seemed to magnetize her. She would buy new clothes made of fine fabrics, putting an end to miserable living, and she would wear these clothes to work.

She easily found—as if fated—a little dress made of a silk fabric the same color as her work blouse. It slid over her body like water. She immediately bought it in case someone else took it, together with some other similar products, handbags and shoes, and she ended up spending all the money she had managed to save.

She didn't care, in fact she felt the opposite; she felt she was flying as she carried the heavy bags back home, panting asthmatically but completely happy. That night she wore her pure silk negligee, low-backed with thin shoulder straps, giving her a sense of sensuality. The same reaction encompassed Kostas, who was not used to sexy appearances, including the highlights in her newly cut hair and her manicure. They did not sleep at all that night while they made love with her wearing her sexy outfit.

"You're really something, you drive me crazy," he sighed as he fell back onto the pillow to catch his breath.

"I have other surprises for you!" Elvina could not keep it to herself.

"What," asked Kostas impatiently.

"I converted all my money into soft fabrics," she did not reveal any more as she wanted him to maintain his fervor since the sex between them had recently waned.

She was just as cheerful the next morning when she put on her pure silk dress and not her work blouse. Everybody looked at her when she appeared at work and took her place behind the cash-register, but no one said anything.

When her boss came in he greeted her, "Good morning! How are you Elvina?" He asked because he knew she had taken sick leave and did not expect a reply. His next question was "Where's your blouse?"

"I thought I'd wear this old thing that was the same color," she said, deriding her dress as much as she could. "I seemed to be allergic to the fabric of the uniform."

"Was this your indisposition? You told us something different," her boss' voice vacillated between anger and irony.

"My migraine may have been allergic." Elvina raised her chin defiantly and pulled open the drawer of the cash-register, indicating that the conversation was over, but she was not the one to end it as she had not started it.

The boss' anger boiled over at her defiant chin and drawer-pulling, agreeing to the conversation stopper but ending it his way, "You come tomorrow wearing your blouse or don't come at all," he concluded and made his way to his office.

"You obviously never went back!" Stefanos grimaced disdainfully at all bosses and their mentality.

"Of course she went back, otherwise she'd have lost her job," the ambulance driver answered him categorically as he knew all about employers.

When did I speak to these two, she asked herself and what exactly did I say? What was happening to her, she was terrified as on the one hand she felt she knew exactly where she was, while at other times she felt lost. She wondered if she actually did go to that wonderful club in Prague with Stefanos or did she imagine it with all its details.

What's happening to me, she asked herself in a panic-stricken mood, which brought about a mocking laugh from the angular face of Nontas as he continued maliciously:

"Don't be scared, we've all passed this phase where we don't know where we are."

"What phase do you mean?" asked Elvina in a frightened tone.

"Forget about him," said Stefanos, throwing him a contemptuous look, "He's all screwed up, he's drunk. He's drunk when he drives the ambulance and has banded together with the paramedics to take a break from transporting patients for a glass of tsipouro or two."

"Watch what you're saying," the driver's face turned red with anger. "This happened once and the person we were transporting was dead to the world. Why should we hurry up and take him to the hospital when we should have taken him straight to the morgue."

"Fair enough," Stefanos' face again took on that cold, motionless expression which infuriated Nontas.

"Don't get me started with the lies you've told us," he threatened Stefanos, but instead of doing it and exposing all the lies expounded by Stefanos, he suddenly disappeared.

Elvina found herself more confused than ever after listening to their verbal slinging match, since her problems were more important that those between the two of them.

"What's happening to me?" she asked rhetorically. "Tell me, what's going on between him and you?" she asked Stefanos with tears ready to pour from her eyes.

"Forget about him," Stefanos immediately shut out Nontas. "He's a drunkard, a nobody who carries all his problems with him. And he has the gall to go against me. Forget him, he's not worth bothering about".

"Anyway, he started the conversation. He complimented you how beautiful you are in your silk clothes. And you in turn, revealed to us your weakness for soft and beautiful fabrics, followed by that despicable boss of yours who forced you to wear that work blouse that made you sick."

"Since you heard it all, what else can I say, I don't remember," in her nervousness Elvina jumbled her words.

"It happens sometimes when someone wants to forget something he rejects it from his mind."

"This was probably what Nontas meant when he said that you all have been through this," concluded Elvina hesitantly, but willing to accept his version. She didn't want to overload her brain with any other explanation as it was already being bombarded with needles filled with new nightmarish events that were trying to enter her brain and she was pushing them away.

"What about Prague? How did I find myself there?" she managed to whisper.

"How childish you are," Stefanos broke out of the frozen shell that had encompassed him and he leaned towards her. "How naive you are," he repeated, substituting the word 'childish' for 'naive'. "We travelled to Prague through my words and my descriptions. We haven't moved an inch out of our pavilion . . . from Eleonora's pavilion."

"Was Eleonora the lady who built it?" Elvina expressed her doubt in order to get away from her own doubts.

"Yes, this is Eleonora's little house," Stefanos resolved her misgivings while putting on the frozen, motionless face that frightened Elvina, asking herself again why was she spending her time with peculiar strangers.

"I never went back to my job," she hastened to change the conversation from the pavilion lady to herself. "I didn't go back to the store," she bragged but her joy was short-lived. "Things took a turn for the worst since then, and even the surprises I had for Kostas were wasted," she ended, her expression saddened by these thoughts. Stefanos cut her off, his eyes shining as if he was crying with dry tears:

"Don't talk to me about surprises since I was always surprising Mara. I would wrack my brain how to impress her and she . . . she at the end shafted me, she gave me the surprise of the century."

"Talk about it! Get it off your chest and maybe I can help you," said Elvina, proposing her well-known fairytale that if you turn your troubles or your mistakes into words, they would stop bothering you. But Stefanos however had already cleared off; he might not have been ready to confess all or he was just avoiding her.

She would leave and never return back to this garden with its strange visitors. The serenity which had initially enveloped her had now turned into thunderstorms. The trees had whispered in the beginning but she had ignored them.

Shivers ran down her spine as she turned around to leave, when the little bald-headed boy ran into her, grabbing her by her long skirt. Today he again had no hair on his head. His grip on her was so strong she could not move.

"You didn't bring me a ball!!" he shouted at her accusingly, repeating it again and again in an ever-increasing strident voice. Elvina covered her ears with her hands to escape his shrieking, dragging him behind her as she could not break his grip from her skirt. What could she say . . . she had not managed to buy the ball because the salesman had ignored her. Not even a small boy would accept this excuse.

"I'll buy you one," she affirmed in between his screaming but the little boy would not stop demanding. Elvina knelt before him, dropping to the level of his head. She reached out to caress his bald head but her hands could not move towards him. Suddenly his head filled with hair, long-brownish-blonde hair that was real hair.

When she again stretched out her hand to pet his hair, tufts of hair came loose in the palm of her hand, entwined between her fingers. A scream escaped her lips, much louder in intensity than those emitted by the small boy, while trying to get rid of the hair that was wrapped around her arm, from her wrist up to her elbow.

The boy brought his small face close to hers and stuck out his huge black tongue at her while pulpy slimy pieces of bile dripped onto her clothes, staining them. She fell down in order to escape him but his head continued to grow in size, continuing to drench her with fluids dripping from his mouth.

"Come here you bad boy, leave the girl alone," a quiet imposing voice was heard, accompanied by a hand that caught the small boy and pulled him away from Elvina. The voice then turned to Elvina, "He's a naughty but oh so sweet boy that I absolutely adore!" She hugged the boy, who now was quiet and cute as all ten-year olds, and cuddled him.

Elvina, who had been lying on the ground, now stood up. Looking at her dress, she saw there were no traces of the stains caused by the youngster's vomit. It seemed as if he had never dirtied it.

"Are you his mother?" she asked the woman who was now addressing the little rascal with endearing words.

"His mother, no I'm not his mother," the woman replied sadly. "I couldn't have children so I'm looking after this little boy. Isn't that right, my boy? Don't the two of us have a good time together? Don't I look after you?" as she hugged him to her bosom.

"No, you don't look after me," the small boy began shrieking again, but at the softer level of a spoilt brat whose every whim is not fulfilled. "You didn't buy me a ball," he continued harping on the same tune.

"You have a lot of balls. Which one should I bring you to play with?" asked the woman, grabbing him by the arm as they slowly disappeared from sight, the small boy continuing to grumble.

Elvina stood up in order to run away and never come back. Near the exit gate she came across Marilena Evangelou.

"I was looking for you," the diva said, stopping her route.

The girl stopped for a moment out of politeness.

"If you play in the show I will tell you whatever you want to learn about love, whatever you're lacking in and I will even pay you well."

"What show?" Elvina managed to articulate in surprise.

"We are playing in the theater that bears my name, you will be playing me in my youth," said the actress as she disappeared into the darkness of the thick vegetation.

Chapter 2

THE SHOW

That which differentiated this attempt to stage a theatrical production from other more usual stage productions was the fact that there was no producer and no specific play. Marilena Evangelou took on the role of producer while the show that was to be presented contained excerpts from her greatest hits and also the star would talk about her life in general, something she had never done before.

Even without the promises of the theatrical diva that she would reveal everything concerning love and that Elvina would be paid—this latter factor was a serious consideration for Elvina, as it would be a lie to say that she was not in need of money—she would have been the first to take part in this play, even without this financial incentive, because this was one of the most significant opportunities ever to have fallen in her lap. An invitation by a star of the stature of Marilena Evangelou to play her young years would be the apex of her life.

A problem that immediately arose was clothes . . . she had nothing to wear except for the dress she wore every day when she went out on her travels. Even though it was a model outfit made from fine silk, she wore it continuously. She could of course wear a light beige colored evening outfit she had bought with the dress that had replaced her supermarket uniform, but she couldn't find where she had hung it. She couldn't find any of her dresses; in fact, all her clothes seemed to have disappeared. Where were all the designer clothes she had bought during the era of Mr. Big, as well as the last few pieces she had purchased with her last savings?

She wracked her brain unsuccessfully, trying to remember where she had hidden them, she just could not imagine where. When she had moved from Kostas' apartment, she was sure she had taken them all to her new place, she would not have left any of her belongings behind, especially clothes made of fine quality fabrics, which were her weakness.

She had not returned to the store following the episode with her boss and she was still mad at Kostas for not supporting her.

"I can't say that it's good for you to wear that damn uniform for eight hours every day, but think about the other girls, each one of them would want to wear whatever she felt like."

"So what! How does uniformity in clothes help?" Elvina retorted, wanting to continue the argument but Kostas thought otherwise.

"Some women prefer it so as not to wear out their own clothes."

"I'm tired of wearing the same thing every day," complained Elvina. How could she demean herself and drop from the velvet palaces of her childhood dreams to the stiff 'cement-orientated' uniform of the supermarket, with a man who did not expect more than that from her? That was when Elvina decided to call her mother.

"My darling, come back to the island, we miss you!" Her mother began to sweet-talk her but she could not return to the island with her head down. And with her coughing on the rise, her parents would again begin the rounds of doctors and medical tests.

"I'll come," she replied, lying through her teeth in order to terminate the conversation and rush off to the beach.

Since it was now summertime, Elvina would hop onto a bus and laze around the coastline instead of wandering around the countryside and the suburbs. She visited all the beaches, the closest ones and the ones further away, sandy beaches and other ones covered with small pebbles. Sun-tanning, swimming in the sea and again the circle. This recipe worked for her so she would end up home late in the evening. Since she was usually hungry at this time, she would cook something and later sit with Kostas, small-talking at the table.

"Today I went to Skinia, the water was divine!" she described her day.

"The air-conditioning broke down at the store," he replied.

"In September I'll start looking for work," Elvina promised, "After the holidays."

They decided to travel around the Cyclades Islands in August, making reservations at two or three islands, as one island was too restrictive for Elvina, she wanted more. The islands were great, the sea refreshing and the beaches overflowing with deckchairs, while the clubs blared out their music. Elvina felt divine in her new ethereal clothes and filled their bed with surprises and lacy underwear, but they were not having a good time.

"I'll return back to the supermarket wearing that coarse uniform," Elvina began one morning as they lazed around in bed.

"No you won't!" replied Kostas.

"It bothers you, doesn't it?" she retorted.

"It's your life," he replied, shrugging his shoulders.

"Aren't we together?" she asked.

"Are we??" he queried, as if asking himself, but neither he nor Elvina answered and the conversation ended on this note.

During the evenings they would sit in a bar looking at the stars and the sea-waves, peaceful and silent, as if the scenery was separating them instead of bringing them together.

"I'm sitting in that boat," said Elvina, expressing the sense of their parting, as she looked at a small boat tugging across the sea, with just a small light showing to protect it from being rammed by a larger yacht.

"What do you mean? Do you want to go on a boat-ride? Kostas replied as he was lost in his thoughts.

"I'm already on the boat," she repeated.

"Stop talking gibberish," he replied angrily. "I'm tired of your bullshit."

But they only broke up about two months after returning to Athens, after Elvina again began hitting the beaches.

She did not care what time she returned home. She would return late at night, around ten in the evening and sometimes even later. She did not of course stay at the beach until that time. Time was lost traveling back and forth, waiting at the bus-stop, getting into the bus, changing buses, and so on.

"Where were you?" Kostas would ask, at first concerned by the late hour.

"In Nea Makri?" she vacillated.

"Are you kidding me?" he answered angrily.

"No, but I'm confused. I think I was in Nea Makri yesterday. Today I went to Kinetta and that's why I am late," she retorted triumphantly.

"Are you hungry? Have you eaten?" he decided to change the subject, since he had returned home before her and found all the pots in the cupboard and the fridge empty, so he had ordered a pizza and beers.

"I was going to pick up something but the bus was late," Elvina replied, trying to justify herself.

"What do you do spending so many hours there?" Kostas asked, jumping from one subject to another.

"The weather was great, the beaches not crowded and the sea clean. Why don't you come with me next time," the young girl proposed.

"Forget it!" he responded, rejecting her suggestion. Besides, he still had to open the bookstore every day. "Are you hungry? There's pizza."

"I'll have a piece," Elvina assented as she went off to shower off the salt from her body.

A few days later—it may even have been even a week as Elvina was not keeping track of time, why should she—she returned home the following morning. She found Kostas pacing back and forth in the kitchen, his eyes red and puffed from lack of sleep, holding a coffee pot in his hand as he filled his cup with coffee. He looked like a hero in the comics, but the hero would be holding a gun in his hands and not a coffee pot, and Elvira just managed to stop herself bursting out in laughter.

"I missed the bus," she explained truthfully. How time had flown, she thought. She had overslept on the sand, the weather had been fine and the night as bright as day. It was late in the evening when she opened her eyes. She quickly gathered up her things but the last bus had just passed by. She was in Lavrio and the buses stopped running after ten in the evening. The only thing she could do was to return to the beach. It was wonderful, the moon had added its luster to the star-lights or maybe she had just not noticed it before in her haste to leave.

"Why do people spend their nights closed in their homes, they just don't know what they're missing," she said as she described the events to Kostas, while he continued to watch her, blurry-eyed and red-faced in anger.

"You probably caught a chill out there," he commented, his voice trembling as it escaped through his teeth. His comments were not far from the truth as the chill had seeped into her early that morning and she had begun to cough again.

It will soon disappear, she thought as she moved towards the bedroom to undress, when she heard Kostas' voice: "That's it! I have had enough!" He was just managing to control the tone of his voice. "Pack up your things and push off."

Elvina now remembered clearly, she herself had packed her clothes in suitcases and the rest of her stuff in hold-alls. She had then left to stay with Sonia, a friend of a friend from the supermarket, who lived alone and was looking for a roommate to share expenses. Elvina had called her as soon as Kostas left for the bookstore. She had known for some time now that their relationship was going nowhere but she was too lazy to end things herself. She knew that she had arrived at Sonia's small apartment with all her things, but where had she put them after that. She just could not find a dress to wear for her theatrical appearance.

"Don't worry," Stefanos tried to calm her down. "We usually wear something all the time, we don't dirty it and we don't wear it out. Look at me! Since you've known me, haven't I worn the same shirt and pants all the time, but they are always clean and freshly ironed, as if I had just worn them. Even though I don't wear the jacket very often, I can easily take it to the theater for rehearsals."

"But my dress is dirty. I wore it every time I came here. I can't, I must change it." But when she looked at herself, she saw that her dress looked brand new, as if she had just bought it at the shops and that it was the prettiest of all her clothes, silk with lace trimming along the hemline and the décolletage. It was just right for the occasion.

"Where is the theater?" a new anxiety crisis arose as soon as the old one had disappeared. "How do we get there, by bus or the metro system? At what station do we get off?"

"Tell me where you live so I can guide you," offered the ambulance driver who had just appeared in front of them out of nowhere. "I know Athens like the back of my hand," he boasted, even though it was natural that as a driver he should know his way around Athens.

"Where do I live?" Elvina spoke out aloud and immediately turned red in embarrassment. They would start teasing her, she sounded so stupid since she couldn't remember where she lived. However, neither Stefanos nor the ambulance driver seemed to exploit this gaffe of hers other than just look at her understandingly. Kostas and she had lived far away from the city centre, that she was sure of, and then she had moved to Ambelokipi to stay with Sonia, but where was she living now? She just didn't know, her mind was a blank which seemed to expand as she tried to remember.

"Come by here and we'll go together," said Stefanos in a soothing and relaxing voice, thus putting an end to her problem.

Everyone was on edge before the meeting for the rehearsals at the 'Marilena Evangelou' Theatre. The only exception was the cripple who continued his idiosyncratic comings and goings, sometimes next to the pavilion and other times along the narrow alleyways under the tall cypress and palm trees. Elvina was now somewhat used to him and his random encounters did not scare her as it did the first time they had met.

"He was not invited by the Diva," concluded Nontas, prancing around because he had been invited. "Hold on a minute," he said as he grabbed the cripple by the arm, forcing him to stand unnaturally still like a statue.

"What do you want?" The cripple turned around expressionless but impatient. Elvina shivered instinctively, she was still scared of him and close-up he seemed more terrifying.

"Do you know anything about Monday night?" The ambulance driver was vague.

"Know what?" The statue did not move nor change the expression on his face.

"Okay, forget it!" replied Nontas, regretting that he had addressed him.

"What's happening Monday night, mate?" He was now a statue with short feet and a pincer-like grasp. As a cripple he depended on his arms and so had developed muscles with increased strength, which now grappled Nontas tightly. Luckily the Diva appeared on the scene and saved Nontas from a worse fate.

"I'm inviting everyone who is interested in taking part in the show that will be held in the theater bearing my name to come to the first meeting on Monday evening," she announced and then looking at the cripple, added, "What can you do?" He let go of Nontas while thinking about her question.

"I walk," he said, as if he was accomplishing something serious, and everyone suddenly noticed his wonderfully deep bass voice.

"You can be the presenter," the Diva immediately gave him his role. "It doesn't matter if you suspend your walking around for a while," she assured him while smiling broadly. Her voice could melt ice and the cripple bowed at her as he said that he would be there, and continued:

"Can I please leave you all to continue my walk?"

The Diva thanked him but Elvina could not hide the fears she felt.

"He will speak behind the curtain without appearing," explained the Diva, reassuring Elvina.

"What is a theater?" asked the small boy who suddenly appeared with a head full of brownish-blond curly hair and a ball in his arms as he rubbed against Elvina's dress like a cat.

"You'll dirty my dress," she said as she pulled away.

"What is a theater? What is a theater?" he yelled shrilly. The Diva who was the most suitable person to answer him was nowhere in sight, so Stefanos undertook to resolve his curiosity.

"It's a place where everything that takes place is not true," was his explanation. The small boy thought about this, feeling somewhat mixed up, and suddenly erupted:

"Why didn't my mom take me there? If she took me to the theater, my illness wouldn't be real. Why didn't she take me there?" he concluded.

"It doesn't work exactly like that," replied Stefanos, trying to correct the uncorrectable.

"She didn't take me because she doesn't love me," the small boy burst into tears while large clumps of hair began falling from his head onto the ground, until he was completely bald. "She loves only my brother. She never wanted me," he said as he continued to cry. "She brought me this ball but I don't want it any more" and he threw it out into the narrow pathway. It began to roll downhill between the flowerbeds. Some children suddenly appeared to grab it, but the small boy ran after them yelling "Stay away from my ball! You can't take it!" He started fighting with them as Stefanos, a small smile curling around his lips, yelled:

"Go on, hit them, the ball is yours so don't let them take it!" but his vocal support was not enough. They were three and the small boy could not beat them all. Stefanos then ran towards them and started pushing them and slapping them, forcing them to flee.

The small boy grabbed his ball with his arms, while at the same time one of the invaders stumbled and disappeared from sight, as if the earth had swallowed him.

Elvina watched the incident and the image of the boys fighting almost made her to burst out laughing, but she stopped, petrified, when the boy disappeared from sight.

"I've taken him under my protection, but don't think he's a good boy," said Stefanos as he returned, flustered and red-faced, referring to the small bald boy without having seen the incident of the other boy being swallowed up by the ground. "His mother keeps on buying toys and everything else imaginable but he never shares them with anyone."

Elvina tried to rally herself before croaking out: "Let's go for a walk." Stefanos glanced at her and agreed. He seemed to be more energetic or was she used to his inflexibility, which she now saw as normal.

Stefanos suddenly turned around and burst out, "Let's get out of here! I can't stand this aroma anymore!"

"From which flower is it coming from?" Elvina asked as she looked around at the countless flowerbeds with their blooming multi-colored flowers and inhaled deeply. "It seems like incense . . ." she declared thoughtfully, "as if it's coming from a church."

"It's because there's no wind today," said Stefanos, trying to explain away the stuffy atmosphere caused by the sluggish winds. It was truly a hot, choking day.

A thought suddenly passed through Elvina's mind, that the dress she was wearing would suck in the smell of the incense and that she was to appear at the theater wearing that same dress.

"Let's go!" said Elvina, pulling him by the sleeve. She now touched him easily, seeking his own contact in return.

"Let's go somewhere else," he proposed, suddenly feeling more alive as they left the park behind them and began walking along the pavement. Elvina walked on the tips of her feet as she looked around her. It had been awhile since she had felt so happy. What excited her immensely was the thought of the theatrical production and the role she would be playing. Stefanos felt more invigorated as he walked away from the scents and shadows of the tall shady trees, as he could now raise his head and look at the sun.

They finally reached a large cosmetics store where the salesladies welcomed their customers by enticing them to try out the different scents of each display stand. Elvina stretched out her wrist but was ignored by the saleslady, who sprayed her scents on another customer. Just as she was getting really mad, Stefanos came to her holding a sample bottle in his hand.

"Try this," he said, spraying her without waiting for her response. It was a heavenly scent. "I had given it to her as a gift and she never went anywhere without it," he said reminiscencing. "I could feel her presence from afar, while my sheets were always enveloped with this aroma . . ." He suddenly stopped talking when he saw a figure drifting through the store, going from one stand to another. She was taller than the other ladies and more imposing, a woman who attracted attention.

"It's her! Let's go!" Stefanos croaked in panic. "Hide me so she won't see me. I'm not ready to meet her."

"Which one do you mean?" Elvina was not sure if he was referring to the tall seductive lady or not.

"Didn't I tell you that I can recognize that aroma a mile away. She's here in the store. I don't want her to see me."

"Is it Mara?" whispered Elvina conspiratorially, while the woman's aroma on her wrist and the fear of the man who swore by her name affected her deeply.

"Let's go!" he pleaded, "I cannot face her now." He managed to leave the store without being seen by hiding behind the other customers. When Elvina finally reached him, he was sitting on a bench further down.

"Am I safe? She didn't come this way, did she?" he asked Elvina as soon as he saw her, withdrawing back into his shell.

"Why the panic? Can't you just say hello?" Elvina never repressed her emotions. If she happened to come across Mr. Big or Kostas, she would greet them. Imagine running away so as not to meet them, but Stefanos was trembling uncontrollably. Is this what passionate love is all about, she asked herself as Stefanos was still lost in himself.

"Okay, so we happened to come across her, you saw her, your emotions ran high but now it's all over," she said, trying to revive him.

"It was so sudden, I just didn't believe she would appear before me. Take me far away from here, Elvina, I just can't stand it," he yelled hysterically, scaring the young girl.

"What's the matter? I just don't understand you." She looked at him as if he was mad, while trying to make him talk.

"This concerns a dead woman. Mara is dead, I killed her!" he erupted, his voice coming from deep inside him, vowels and consonants pouring out of his mouth onto his clothes and onto the bench as if they were blobs of blood, pulpy and viscous, staining the ground around him.

"It's her blood," he now murmured. "She appeared seeking vengeance to punish me because I am walking around a free man. I'm hiding in the park from the police. They would never think of finding me there, but she managed to find me."

Elvina drew back, not knowing how to react. His words however shed light to his continuous presence in the garden, which could not otherwise be explained. What was a young man doing there, relating to children, cripples and elderly visitors to the area?

She wanted more details so she asked him to tell her everything. To talk about all the blood and guilt that was trapped inside him and which he could not bear it anymore.

"I killed her," he repeated, "Afterwards I tried to kill myself with the same gun. The first bullet hit her in the abdomen, which is why she lost so much blood. You see, I had never held a gun in my hand before so I did not know where to shoot her. Instead of hitting the heart, the first bullet penetrated her abdomen, while the second entered her arm before she fell down. She lurched around until the third bullet caught her in the neck as she fell, sinking into her own blood."

Elvina remained speechless as she moved back to avoid the blood creeping on the ground towards her shoes, and she now stammered in shock.

"So much blood, why did you kill her, you kept on saying how much you loved her? You bought her perfumes, you took her abroad . . ."

"I took her everywhere. I've mentioned just a few of the things I did for her, I lived only for her. I would go to sleep and wake up thinking only of her . . . and she shafted me."

"What happened? Did she leave you?" Elvina suffered with him, her emotions wracking her body as she looked at Stefanos collapsing onto the bench. How could such a young man give so much at such an early age and end up mourning on the small bench on the street, while hiding in the jungle of the densely vegetated garden.

"What happened?" she asked again, curious to find out how he ended up there.

"We were planning to get married," he said, deciding to speak out. "I wanted to marry her as soon as possible, while she counter-proposed that summer on an island. Summer was still a long time away and I was impatient. She told me why worry since we were together, she comforted me. I insisted that we get married tomorrow, wherever she wanted—here, abroad, on an island, wherever she wanted—but I finally agreed to the summer. We began to look at the islands to choose one with a small church, to celebrate with friends, it wasn't bad. When we were apart and I had an idea, I would text her to her cell-phone, "Let's get married on Amorgos." It doesn't feel right, she replied.

I reminded her that we had gone there on our first holidays together, but the island was not of her choice. So Amorgos was out but this didn't bother me because her refusal opened up new horizons for us to seek. I would quickly finish my work and then surf the Internet for remote and mystical places, unknown beaches and small out-of-the-way islands."

"I used to leave home and hit all the coastlines, leaving behind men, jobs, weddings, children, recognition and who knows what else," Elvina interrupted him to narrate her own experiences. But Stefanos dumbfounded her in his quiet manner:

"If you loved him it would have been different. Whatever you mentioned scornfully I consider them to be heavenly." He articulated his last word as slowly as possible, as if projecting an image of enchantment in front of them, but he did not maintain this as he continued on by changing his last words in a hoarse voice. "They would have resembled either a dream or a nightmare," and his facial features took on the horrific grimace of a man who had shot his lover three times.

"What made you go so far?" insisted Elvina.

"While I was looking for perfection in our relationship, she stabbed me in the back." His voice was so harsh and rigid she could not recognize the tender young man of before. "She had an affair with my best friend, we grew up together, we played football in the same open ground before they erected an apartment building there. He stole my girlfriend, how did they manage it without me noticing? I was such a fool.

We would pick up Tony—that was his nickname for Anthony— because he was down in the dumps as he had broken up with his girlfriend, so we went to take him out as he was crying his heart out. Now he's certainly crying his heart out because I killed him too," a croak erupted from Stefanos' throat that could have been a laugh.

"You killed him as well, I don't believe it?" Elvina said in a surprised tone.

"I kept the other bullets for him. I turned the gun towards him. The first bullet passed by to his left shoulder without hitting him, the second entered his chest and was the decisive one. I then swiveled the gun around and fired a third time, which just missed my shoulder."

"I don't believe it," Elvina had nothing else to say.

"I killed him as well, he deserved it!" Stefanos withdrew back into his shell, closed his eyes and refused to say another word, despite Elvina's entreaties for confirmation of what he had just confessed to. It was only after some time that Stefanos spoke again, parrot-wise, repeating the same phrase over and over again.

"This was my destruction with her death and that of my friend," he murmured incoherently until his voice and his body disappeared from the bench, leaving Elvina wondering how he managed to vanish like a shadow. His words of course explained why he was always in the park, hiding from everyone, but he had seen the dead woman, or damned by his guilt he imagined that he had seen the woman he had pointed out to Elvina.

Elvina was not sure which woman he was talking about, there were so many attractive customers in the crowded store looking to tone up their good looks with cosmetics and perfumes.

However, after this incident Elvina would never have set foot in the green-filled garden if it wasn't for the show, as the allurement of this invitation was huge. This was an invitation she could not and would not ignore.

So she was there Monday afternoon, just as dusk was falling and daylight was not competing with the lamps whose luminance could just be seen among the green-black Cypress trees. An idyllic moment that Elvina would normally have enjoyed, but the presence of Stefanos, who was waiting to accompany her to the theatre, was frightening.

"He's a murderer and a fugitive," she whispered into Nontas' ear, who was wandering around.

"Stefanos? Don't worry about it, just forget it."

"How can I," the young girl wondered, "He's killed two people, isn't that awful?"

"So he kidded you as well? Don't take it seriously as maybe it didn't happen that way." Nontas added the word 'maybe' but his expression stated that he was sure it was not true.

Elvina tried to insist but at that moment Stefanos joined them, expressionless and apathetic, telling them they should leave for the theater.

"Everyone will be there, so we should also go."

They strolled out through the gate and arrived at the theater without Elvira in her bewildered state realizing it.

The stage was dominated by the Theatrical Diva, wearing her long dress with its lace trimming, her high-heeled sandals and her wide hat. Her clothes had impressed Elvina from the very first moment. She had thought then that they were so old-fashioned, but now she realized they were theatrical clothing.

"This was Blanche DuBois' costume in one of her greatest hit shows and that's why she's wearing it," explained Stefanos, who had noticed her wonderment.

Marilena Evangelou chose that moment to stand up and bow before beginning to speak. It did not take her long to give her instructions, which were simple and brief. She would be playing excerpts from some of her most famous roles while the presenter would announce her from behind the quints. In between she would talk about her life as everyone wanted to know the details of her personal life.

She was finally breaking her silence, and here the dots in her phrases were expressed with such expertise, everyone listening to her fantasized her walking down a shady tree-lined road accompanied by a tall gentleman. Some saw him with dark hair and others with brownish hair whispering in her ear.

"I will reveal all my secrets," she said finally, with everyone showing rapt attention except Nontas, who whispered into Elvina's ear.

"I wonder what she's up to, what's on her mind?"

"Shush," she gestured as she waited to hear the details of her participation.

The Diva apportioned the roles as follows: the cripple with the bass voice would present the show, Elvina and Stefanos would portray the Diva and her lover during her youth, when she would make the much anticipated revelations, while general duties would be undertaken by Nontas and the woman who looked after the small boy since she herself had no children. They would be responsible for everything, from the various theatrical sets up to the seats themselves.

The theater itself would be filled to capacity as all the visitors to the park were invited. As for the tickets—here a smile escaped her lips which seemed to caress them as a positive aura blowing both joy and energy—the price would be a rose, a gardenia or a carnation.

Let them bring whatever flower they wanted, the area itself was overflowing with flowers, and again her wonderful laugh filled the air.

"What a woman! said Elvina admiringly.

"What a cajoler! grumbled Nontas, the show's general duties man as everyone began to disband in order to reassemble for the rehearsals. But . . .

"I'm not moving an inch from here," squealed the small bald-headed boy, sitting in a seat in the front row and holding a ball that was different from the usual ones he held in his hands. "I'm staying here" in a more strident voice, while the woman who looked after him went to remove him from his seat. "I brought my new ball and I'm staying here," while continuing suddenly, "This is a theater, isn't it?" not really knowing what a theater was.

"Yes it is," the Diva assured him, engrossed in her own matters, probably thinking how she would program the rehearsals and organize the show.

"Since this is a theatre I'm not budging," his voice now whining. "I'm not leaving because everything here is not real, that's what Stefanos said," the small boy was trying to explain why he was so insistent. "As long as I'm here, I won't be sick. I'm fine and I brought my new ball."

He got up from his seat to bounce his ball on the carpet that covered the floor of the theatre.

Everyone looked in amazement at the small boy who believed he would regain his health. They shivered involuntarily while the small boy began to kick his ball. He suddenly patted his head, "My hair has grown again," showing everyone his rich mane of hair. "Didn't I tell you all, I'm in the theater and they will never fall off again. I am healthy so I will never need chemotherapy again."

As he uttered these last words, he began to pull his hair to prove the miraculous effects of the theater, but tufts broke off between his fingers. The small boy looked in bewilderment at his fingers full of hair from his head, looking firstly at his fingers and then at the other people around him, confused and desperate and unable to utter another word until he suddenly became hysterical while pointing his finger at Stefanos.

"You lied to me! My mother won't let me tell lies!" and he began to cry.

"What's going on? The actress asked Stefanos to explain.

"He asked me what the theater was," Stefanos replied quietly and melancholically, his voice just audible above the screams of the small boy. "He didn't know what it was, he had never been to one, he had never heard of it. I told him it was a make-believe world. How could I imagine that he would believe that if he came here his illness would prove to be false and he would be healthy as before . . . a healthy boy without any problems," he explained desperately.

Elvina wondered how many of those present were like the small boy, hoping for a miracle, something that would take them back. Her heart filled with tenderness for Stefanos and she held his hand, leaving behind her all that he had confided to her concerning the savage murders.

"Stefanos is full of lies, don't listen to him," Nontas spoke in a strong voice as he approached the small boy to boost his morale.

"It's not a lie," interrupted the Theatrical Diva as she moved towards the small boy who in his perplexity seemed to hear her. "Sit here and you'll forget everything. That's what I did. As soon as I went on stage I would forget everything else," she concluded and then withdrew back into her shell. The restless expression on her face transformed into an immovable wall, but she again opened up for the sake of the small boy. "Stay here as long as you want, play in the hall, climb up onto the stage, chase after your ball, no one will stop you."

The small boy looked at her without really understanding what she meant, since he was still feeling miserable, but he would like to do what she proposed, as the others began to depart.

"No!" He raised his head up emphatically, still completely bald while the skin on his cranium emphasized the bones of his head. "No, I'll come with you. My mother will be looking for me. She won't find me if I stay here and I want to see her, I want my mother," he began crying as the woman who cared for him hugged him as they moved towards the exit.

"My ball! My ball!" the small boy cried out suddenly as he broke away from her to find his ball.

Elvina laid her hand on Stefanos' hand and left it there. She didn't care if he was a murderer and a fugitive, or maybe this was the reason why she was more attracted to him. At one point, when everyone's attention had been drawn to the small boy and his tantrums, Stefanos squeezed her hand and they walked away with lowered heads. Each one was engrossed in his or her own thoughts, walking along without paying any attention if there was any cars and pedestrians on the road, and they suddenly found themselves outside the gates of the park.

Elvina would not leave him alone, he was a child just like the small boy who caused the ruckus at the theater, a child that had destroyed his life, if what he had confided in her was true.

"Don't think about it," she squeezed his arm more tightly to draw his attention. "Gone and forgotten," she ruminated.

"It's when I saw her," Stefanos stammered, "When I saw her everything came to mind."

"Let's go to the pavilion," proposed Elvina to take his mind off this unpleasantness and it worked. Stefanos raised his head as a smile seemed to flitter across his face and he responded to her squeeze by squeezing her hand back.

"The lily that was budding is now flowering," he informed her as to what was happening in their pavilion, "A small yellow flower like Tweety," and they laughed together.

"I have never loved anyone, nor has anybody loved me back up to now," the young girl complained in the pavilion of love, hoping for some sympathy. But Stefanos, instead of comforting her, withdrew back into his shell again after a brief period of humaneness, showing a face with a tough impenetrable exterior which Elvina did not notice as she was all wrapped up in her own affairs.

"Mr. Big had charmed me," she remembered, "but it was a lost cause. At times Kostas would raise my spirits but other times he would drag me down to the level of feeling superficial and mad."

"Maybe you weren't?" he interrupted her in a serious tone, forcing her to admit it.

"I still am since I'm still wandering from place to place," Elvina agreed bitterly. Stefanos did not reply as he absent-mindedly stroked the leaves of the nearby bushes while the young girl carried on sighing: "I left Kostas as I left Mr. Big and before them my parents and my studies.

After leaving Kostas, I went to stay with Sonia to share expenses. Since then I've gone from bad to worse, from one job to another, from one man to another. And there's of course my cough, which has deteriorated, sending me twice to the hospital. The first time was the reason I lost my job," she laughed self-pityingly and continued her explosive flashbacks.

Her employer had been forced to take her to hospital when she had suffered a coughing asthmatic attack. She could not breathe, all the blood left her face and she felt she would faint right there in the shop, how could she wait for Nontas' ambulance. She laughed wanly without speaking as she made the association. She was lucky he had taken her immediately to the hospital, where they kept her for two weeks, discharging her with prescriptions for medicines and lots of advice. She should come in periodically for observation, she should not tire herself and she should eat well.

Did she follow this advice? Of course not. At her job she stood all day from morning to night. The only job she could find with her qualifications was as a salesgirl, nothing more. At the supermarket she may have worn the Gestapo-styled uniform but at least she had her chair behind the cash register. But all this was in the past.

So her only defense now was, when she woke up in the morning dead tired from work and late nights to look for another job instead of going back to the same work. In any event, Athens has innumerable shops and she herself was presentable and polite with customers when she was not bored with them. "Blue is your color, you should only wear blue," she would say and she actually meant it when she would look critically at a woman trying on a blue dress; she did have perception and good taste.

It was great when she was hired as a make-up artist. Customers preferred her as she was an artist with lipsticks, shades and tints, eye shadows, eyebrow contouring, why the hell did she leave that job? She wracked her brain trying to remember the reason but nothing came to mind, it couldn't have been serious as she would then have remembered it.

Suddenly she remembered, she had left a good customer sitting for hours while she was engrossed in the classical statuette face of a young lady who was looking for the perfect make-up for her wedding ceremony.

"Elvina, you're working too slowly," her boss warned her. "Elvina, working at this rate we'll all be out of a job," he yelled, hoping to snap her out.

"Okay, I'm finishing," she said, trying to reassure him. But then she had the urge to try out a new make-up scheme, which took her another thirty minutes, resulting in the customer stomping out of the store in a rage, slamming the door behind her. She was soon followed by the make-up artist that was Elvina, fired by her boss.

"I want to do great things," Elvina confided to her roommate Sonia one night after they had bathed and were drying their hair in front of the mirror.

"What kind of things?" asked Sonia inattentively as she tried to comb one of her curls.

"It's hard to say," Elvina just couldn't express what she wanted to say. "I want to fall in love, I want to paint," stating two completely different abstracts.

"It seems that this has remained from your make-up days," said Sonia, emphasizing the second abstract and concluding that since Elvina was good wielding make-up brushes she wanted to try her talents wielding paint brushes.

"I want to paint portraits," said Elvina, continuing her dream, "Portraits that would display the soul of the person I was painting."

"Nobody wants his soul bared for all to see," Sonia replied, trying to put an end to this.

"You I will paint with your tongue sticking out," Elvina responded without thinking.

"Why?" was all that her friend managed to say in surprise.

"Because you are a glutton for everything!" laughed the future artist. It was true that Sonia ate a lot and did many things. She was a sales representative for a company selling consumer goods and killed herself trying to sell her products and reach her sales target in order to win her bonus. She had a boyfriend whom she left when he lost his job, but she soon replaced him with a handsome dude with his own store. Sonia would help out at the store in her free time. They had a great time going away for weekends, making love during the day, lots of friends and going out all night whenever the opportunity arose, while Elvina would be sleepy and bored, spending her time sitting in front of the television.

This happened frequently as she would be tired from work, so she quit her job. That was when she had a bright idea and soon found a new man similar to Mr. Big. It didn't take long before she asked him for a loan to pay her rent until she could find another job. The trick worked, so she repeated with her next affair.

Sonia did not approve this way of life but she still accepted Elvina's share of the rent and other house expenses. In any event, it was what they had agreed upon. But in the middle of the month a new bout of coughing hit Elvina and her temperature rose. She was quickly transported to the hospital on oxygen.

"Maybe I drove you to the hospital, doll-face? Your face seems familiar." Nontas the ambulance driver looked at her inquisitively when they bumped into each other as she roamed the streets wrapped up in her problems. The young girl soon remembered that she had spent some time in hospital. She brought back the memory of the cough tearing her body apart while cold sweat dampened her hair and forehead when she tried to breathe.

Those were bad times but now it was better, she felt fine, she had not coughed in a long time and she now breathed normally and tirelessly. So with lifted spirits she began talking to Nontas.

"How could I see if you were in the ambulance? Does yours have oxygen?"

"Of course it does, even though it doesn't work all the time. Sometimes the valve works, sometimes it sticks. However, you do remind me of a girl who passed through my ambulance."

"The young girl who pretended to be dying?" This was the story he had told her when they had first met.

"It was surely her or some other girl, all you pretty girls look alike, slimly built with long hair. You all have the same figure, but I prefer other types of women, like that one there."

He pointed to a well-built woman with strong thighs wearing flat stout shoes sized at least a forty-two, with black hair collected back in a bun. As she approached them, Elvina noticed a large nose, thick eyebrows and a mole on her cheek.

"Hi doll," the thin bird-like man greeted her.

Despite her bulk, the woman passed by them, walking gracefully, without Elvina having to move out of her way in the narrow street. She winked at Nontas, pleased with his compliment.

It's a wonder she didn't run into me, thought Elvina, while Nontas licked his lips in wonderment.

"I like her, a real woman with everything in the right place," he continued, pointing to the barely discernable woman twenty meters away. The area suddenly filled with figures that made Elvina shiver, probably because of the silence and lack of noise.

"She's a real doll who will crush you in bed," Nontas whistled to her. "Every woman has her attributes, but all you beautiful lassies are the same . . . skinny and arrogant. However, the girl that resembled you was a real piece, petite as they say, a girl like a cherry who was placed into the ambulance with her wrists cut. She was at death's bed, how could we stop the hemorrhaging. Sitting next to her holding her hand was a healthy image of the girl, we thought they must have been twins.

'My darling sister,' bawled the healthy twin, 'Why did you do it?'

'Because I had no name, everyone called me by your name, everybody thought I was you because you were first in everything, you managed to do everything, I couldn't do anything right. I achieved nothing,' and the one who cut her wrists starting crying. She could't have lived, her body was completely dry.

'That wasn't the reason, my darling sister. It was because we were identical and no one could determine which sister was which,' the healthy twin tried to persuade her as to the opposite and bring her back to life. However the suicide twin was not convinced.

'You were the one that always stood out . . .' and that was when she passed away. Tell me, did you ever have a twin sister?" Nontas finished his story with an unexpected and personal question.

"Why do you ask?" replied Elvina in surprise. "No I didn't," she assured him, there was no reason to make a scene.

"Then why doll-face, are you suicidal?"

"Me suicidal?" Elvina was both scared and at the same time misjudged. "Why do you think that . . . me kill myself. I who want to do so much, fall in love, walk through unknown areas, wander around without caring if I lose myself."

She was now lost in the jungles she lusted to cross. How would Nontas notice what she was saying as he was looking as if not listening to her confession. But as she returned from the tropical jungles she continued, "I want to do a lot of important things, I have a lot of time in front of me and I feel great!" She inhaled slowly and deeply in order to enjoy the invigorating air she was taking in. She felt happy, as if she had never been sick and plagued by her respiratory system.

A voice was then heard arising from the bushes surrounding an abandoned monument

"Hey dude, do you have what I asked you for?" the voice addressed Nontas, as a male figure appeared with greasy tousled grey hair and beard that hid the rest of his characteristics and the body of someone who was bent over, ready to take one step forward and two steps back.

"No I don't have it and I don't drink, so bug off," Nontas was angry that his conversation with Elvina had been interrupted and so was ready to pick a fight with the newcomer. "What do you want whiskey for? Haven't you learnt your lesson?"

"No, I'm still searching," the bent figure whined as he backtracked to escape Nontas' assault. "Oh if I only just had a glass," trying to arose Nontas' emotions. "Do something dude," he insisted as if begging.

"Haven't you had enough with all that you've guzzled!" the former ambulance driver roared.

"As soon as my old woman slammed the door behind her I went to the supermarket and filled the boot of my car with bottles," he whined as he turned to the young lady. "A boot filled with bottles. I could never imagine this, not even in my wildest dreams. To avoid her nagging I would hide the bottle under my jacket or deep inside my pocket. I finally crossed myself that I will have some peace and quiet and overfilled the car with booze. I just managed to take one swig from the bottle and here I am. Cross my heart and hope to die, that's what happened. I'm thirsty Nontas, can you find me some?"

"You drank half a bottle without coming up for air and drove your car off the cliff, and you still want more," Nontas said, trying to get rid of him.

"What happened," Elvina asked uncertainly.

"The lad here was so happy to escape from his wife who would not let him drink and had finally left him, he filled his car with bottles but couldn't wait to go home and start drinking. He began while driving on the road, steering wheel and a swig, stamping on the gas and the brake pedals with the bottle in his mouth, and here he is straight from the hospital to complement the party," Nontas began to guffaw but Elvina was getting used to him so she was able to respond.

"Stefanos told us you also drive on the highways in a drunken state."

"You believe this liar who doesn't know what's happening to him," Nontas said angrily as he turned towards Elvina. "I only had one tsipouro for the road, the truck-driver was the one who lost control and hit me head on. One day I'll run into him and smash his face," and he disappeared down the road with his head hung low, just like the previous guy who—feeling disappointed—had in the meantime disappeared into the darkness.

What Elvina remembered clearly about the performance—as if all the scenes were passing before her inside a crystal ball that magnified all the distorted characteristics of those in the middle, while shrinking and blurring the figures oscillating in the wings—was her own participation and the fateful event that took place. She could barely remember the rest, including Marilena Evangelou's fantastic interpretation of various classical roles from her theatrical repertoire. She began with Blanche DuBois, continued with Lady Macbeth and Mother Courage and concluded with what? She ended with one of her greatest hits but Elvina just could not remember what it was.

The audience erupted when she, Elvina, appeared on stage, not because she is a great actress or because her role was difficult, it was because she portrayed the great diva in her youth.

She should have guessed that Marilena Evangelou wanted her for this reason only. That's why she chose Elvina, inundating her with compliments and promises, and now that she rehashes it again in her mind, the Theatrical Diva had emphasized this from the first moment.

"I want you to portray me when I was your age because we look so much alike, it's as if I see myself in you." These were the exact words the star had stated. She never recanted them and repeated them in other words at every opportunity. "Elvina, I had exactly the same dress," she said when they met at the rehearsal, "Where did you find it?" she asked curiously.

"I adore fine fabrics and that's why I went to Monastiraki, that's where you'll find real silk or linen," replied the young girl.

"Aiolou Street has the best shops and that is where I used to go when I did not bring them directly from Paris," the actress said, remembering the past. "I used to buy whole bolts of fabrics, come let me show you my wardrobe, they keep them in the storerooms of the theater," she grabbed Elvina's hand and they went from the stage to the backstage of the theater in absolutely no time.

"Turn on the lights to admire my clothes, I don't need them and anyway, I just can't stand them off-stage and without make-up. It feels great when you are onstage under the powerful spotlights. As the leading lady I would always stand opposite the central spotlight while the adjacent ones would also focus on me. Imagine the hall full of people, completely silent and motionless while I would act my role under the spots. The spotlights would follow me whenever I moved, but I got to hate it, as if they did it on purpose in order to highlight the smallest wrinkle on my face," she ended sadly, but gradually her voice sweetened, as if make-up was being applied to her skin.

"Don't take me seriously when I get mad. It's my temperament, I just can't see myself getting old," she ended and changed the subject by showing off her clothes one-by-one while mentioning in which theatrical production she had worn them. 'Romeo and Juliette' was the first, a gorgeous dress with an embroidered bust, and moved on to

'Sweet Bird of Youth' with its heavy dark silk costume. "This costume left its mark at that time," she sighed wistfully.

"What will I wear for the show?" Elvina wanted to know.

"Yours of course, didn't I tell you I had a similar outfit? Exactly the same with trimming and lace along the hemline, and wearing this you are me. Do you know how long I have waited to meet a girl that looks like me. This is how I was at your age, exactly like you . . . slim, pale, fragile." Her tone was nostalgic, you couldn't tell whether she was telling the truth, lying or just acting, or whether the theater and its lies were her truth. Elvina shivered as she thought about it.

"No, you will not be wearing one of these dresses. Since you will be portraying me, you will be appearing in your dress which is similar to mine," and Elvina agreed silently. "This is how I was, just like you," repeated the actress and continue angrily, "When you grow old you are doomed to walk around as an old woman," she said snipping at herself.

"Marilena Evangelou filled with wrinkles, with sparse hair and aged hands," showing off the upper parts of her palms with their spots and swollen veins. "An old woman's hands, an old woman's body," she added, raising her skirt slightly and lowering it immediately, filled with rapid rage. "Marilena Evangelou doomed to be an eternal old hag," she tottered, making Elvina run into the corner behind the hangers holding the dresses, blouses and hats.

"Luckily you came along," she said as she hugged the frightened young girl. "Don't tremble my darling, if you only knew how many years I've been expecting you, a girl that resembles me," her words now took on a musical tone as her aged fingers lightly caressed Elvina's face and body and she concluded, "I have been waiting for a girl who looked like me to play me at your age."

The conversation soothed Elvina, allowing her to sleep like a baby, something she had not done in a long time. When she was with Kostas, he would wake her up as he rolled around in his sleep, snoring loudly which made Elvina want so much to run away, a feeling that made her get out of bed and walk around as if it was daytime already.

"Aren't you scared of wandering around deserted places?" he tried to stop her.

"I'm not scared of the dark," replied Elvina.

"What about night walkers—thieves, knife-welders, perverts—who might hit on you?" Kostas continued, trying to make her see reason.

"You mean desperate people? They know me, I'm okay with them," as she smiled mysteriously at him, making him break out with pimples.

"When one day something bad happens to you, remember me," and here the conversation ended until they broke up. But no one ever harmed her or badgered her, not even now in the shaded garden. If he could see me know, she scowled, he would freak out. She continued thinking along the same lines as she walked down the narrow roads.

When she broke up with Kostas, it was the coughing that kept her awake. She would wake up two three times during the night feeling she was drowning and she would cough until she calmed down. Luckily Sonia slept soundly and did not realize what was happening. But the strange thing was that she hardly coughed when she was with a man, maybe she was afraid he might leave her. She racked her brains but could not remember an occasion when she coughed in front of a man, but she did not have a good time with them.

Elvina could hardly stand the man who gave her money for her rent or the boy her age whom she had met in a cafeteria one afternoon when she was drinking her frappe coffee with her tears. He lasted a week.

She ended up sleeping restlessly with one man or another, and it seemed that they tired her out.

She would wake up in the morning feeling like hell instead of feeling well and happy. The words of the actress however raised her spirits, giving her the satisfaction of ending up sleeping like a baby that rested her and invigorated her. She hadn't felt this good in years. Just imagine, the Theatrical Diva had been waiting for her . . . an anonymous young girl whose life till then had been down in the dumps. Elvina now shined with pride as she went to meet the Diva.

She found the star barefooted, washing her feet under the cold running water of a tap. There were quite a few taps used for watering the flowers and washing the monuments.

Stefanos had told her, as they wandered around, that the taps were necessary, "For the flowers and trees as well as for the pigeons that drank the water, even though later they would fly very low and dirty the area with their feathers and their droppings".

"These damn birds get on my nerves," Nontas indignantly voiced his opinion about the pigeons.

"They don't bother me," contradicted Stefanos coolly.

"Luckily we have so much water, they would've polluted us to death," insisted Nontas.

But now the actress was using the water to wash her bare feet, sitting on a ledge and letting the icy crystallized water droplets flow onto her white soles. The water-drops shining in the sun resembled pearls while the soles of the Diva that were spread out looked like little pixies.

"Look at my toes," speaking tenderly about her toes, soft and rosy like a little girl. "Only these do not age, they have remained the same since I was a child."

Finishing her phrase she looked thoughtful at the only part of her body that had not betrayed her. Her toes were truly silky and petite, ageless. "It's the only part of my body that has not aged," she confessed calmly as if she was talking about a stranger.

"I have spent half my life in front of a mirror," she admitted nostalgically, "I would rehearse my roles in front of the mirror, as well as my movements, my grimaces that accompanied my words, my body stature and the expressions in my eyes. I would put on my make-up in front of the mirror, change my eye-shadows and lipstick colors to find the ones that suited my role and my interpretation. Do you know that the correct make-up is decisive for the successful rendition of a character? I will teach you everything," she concluded as she removed her feet from the water and asked Elvina to help her put on the old-fashioned sandals she always wore.

"I would spend hours in front of the mirror looking at myself and I know, I'm absolutely certain that you are the same as me as I was at your age. This resemblance is uncanny, it's as if we are sisters," and she laughed bitterly. "Don't look at me as I am now, stop looking at me, you are making me mad. Then we had the same poise, the light pace, the shiny pale skin, so fragile and poignant, just like you. My patience was finally rewarded. As soon as he sees you he'll think I'm me and he'll become all mine, he'll be begging me on his knees."

Her voice was now hard, brittle, and colder than the marble of the monument situated next to her. It was a voice that chilled Elvina so much she was speechless and couldn't ask the Theatrical Diva exactly what she meant when she repeated what she had said before but with greater emphasis.

"He will become mine, he will drop to his knees as soon as he sees you. He will think I'm me and I will dominate him, the scoundrel thought he could get away from me, thinking he can resist me."

"Who are you talking about?" Elvina finally managed to utter the words, letter by letter, she had been so subjugated by the intensity of the Diva.

"You will see who he is, you will see and understand, you will feel what love is, what love is without words, stories and teachings." The actress chuckled out aloud, her mouth wide open while wrinkles formed spider-webs on her cheeks, disappearing deep into the corners of her eyes. Her face transformed into a mesh of evilness dripping bile from the huge open mouth, while a ball of wild hair escaped her hair and stuck onto the open mouth, becoming a pulpy mass.

"You will feel what passion is, what love is," the huge mouth spat out these wonderful words like curses, forcing Elvina, who was sweating profusely, to walk to the tap, fill her cupped hands with water and drench her forehead.

"What happened to my little darling?" asked the Theatrical Diva as she approached Elvina, who wanted to run away, but the woman that was asking her was the renowned Marilena Evangelou, aged but always wonderful and radiant, a star who immediately won her over. She would drink the water the great actress cupped in her hands. The water was scented with wild rose petals that reddened the cheeks of the young girl. Elvina couldn't even remember her terror and the Medusa that appeared before her.

"Come let me tell you your role," she said as she pulled Elvina into an isolated corner.

The theatre hall was packed and dark, with only the red emergency lights shining.

"I have never seen so many people," Marilena Evangelou confessed to Elvina behind the velvet curtains of the stage, the latter suffering stage-fright before her performance in the show as she rubbed herself against the curtains. It was as if she was back in the magical palaces of her childhood where she grew up inside the silkiness of her dreams . . . she with the velvety-sounding name.

"How beautiful they are," said Elvina, admiring the curtains she was leaning against.

"The capacity of the theatre is 600 seats, but today there are people standing in the aisles," the Theatrical Diva was surprised by this deluge of people. As was expected, the park honored her with its presence, there were only a very few that did not turn up at the theater tonight.

Wearing clothes ranging from 'in style' to outdated, some women Elvina's age arrived with tight skirts and high-heeled shoes.

"Chic ladies, where have you been hiding?" was Nontas' only comment.

Mature ladies and gentlemen continued to arrive, wearing clothing tailored many years ago. Everyone held a flower in their hands, which was the ticket to enter the theater, waving them as they waited silently for the show to commence. The small boy with the bald head arrived with a ball cradled in his hands, not a new one but rather an old one which was his favorite.

Stefanos was Elvina's partner, the show's leading man chosen by Marilena Evangelou to portray her loved one.

"Which loved one? She just loves herself." Nontas had again found his bile-filled tone.

"Hold on, wiseass, there are some things that have escaped you," Elvina said mysteriously as the soft velvet curtains on which she had leaned made her feel somewhere between a witch and a fairytale princess.

As for Stefanos, he would not demean himself by changing his expression to either verify or disprove the existence of a loved one, despite the fact that he was playing this specific role.

The clapping in the complete darkness of the theater remained indelibly in the mind of Elvina, but she could only deduce it because the clapping was completely noiseless. What made her deduce this—which at the same time frightened her—was the waving of the flowers caused by the hands clapping. However, the air currents that were created were cold and hair-raising, so when she finally appeared on stage, her body was shaking. If it wasn't for the soft, warm velvet tableau curtains whose folds calmed her beating heart and the stirring glare of the Theatrical Diva, she would have hidden among the velvetings that flowed downwards richly and endlessly, but she did finally go on stage.

The powerful central spotlight, guided by Nontas, focused on Elvina as soon as she stepped onto the stage. She felt the bright light warming her and her spirits rose as she reached the center of the stage to the sounds of an old song she had first heard during rehearsals. The song was melodious, heard with the image of Elvina wearing the dress of a bygone era, with trimming and lace along the hemline, while her hand pushing her long hair away from her face was both calculated and characteristic of the Theatrical Diva.

Whenever Marilena Evangelou approached the flashlights of the photographers, the first thing she did was to sweep the hair from her face, bringing to centre stage her forehead, eyes and lips. "I played with my hands, hair, expressions, movements, a little pouting of the lips, a strong look, and most of the time I did not even have to say a word. I just emitted an aura," which Elvina had tried to duplicate during rehearsals, when suddenly, a roar was heard from the audience.

"Marilena, is that you? I don't believe it!" The voice was heard loud and strong in the silence of the hall with its good acoustics and the melody winding down to its soft conclusion.

For a moment Elvina thought that the movement of her hands collecting her hair was perceptible as well as visual, but the voice was really something . . . amazed, intense in sound and rich in ambience and feeling.

"Marilena, is that you?" the voice repeated, sounding somewhat aged when Elvina heard it a second time. A tall upstanding man, despite his age, passed from darkness into light and stood next to her.

"Nikos, you recognized me?" A whisper was heard from the depths of the stage. Some may have thought that Elvina had spoken, but it was Marilena Evangelou.

"You're the same as when we were together, exactly like that day when we were walking in the countryside. So many years have passed. You have taken me back so many years . . ."

"You had brought me a bouquet of wild violets and later you asked me to go with you and pick some more in the fields. It was spring and nature was full of anemones, lilies, violets and whatever else was blooming in the green grass. You warned me to be careful where I walked, it was a small branch that tomorrow would be budding, and here and there and further down until I did not know where to continue . . ." The voice of the actress throbbed with emotion, in contrast to the man's short powerful voice, her words pronounced slowly, like a young girl just learning to sweet-talk. Even though her body had aged, her vocal chords could still pronounce the words as if she was Elvina's age.

"Marilena, I don't know what to say, you've taken me back so many years . . ." his sharp voice leaving his phrase unfinished while a wave of emotions arising from the audience swept over the stage.

"We used to collect armfuls of flowers and I would then place them into the vases you had filled with water, a vase by the window, a small one on the nightstand next to the bed that filled the room with the scent of violets all night long, which suited my aroma."

"Marilena, what monologue are you presenting?" asked the man since the interpretations of her roles had been performed earlier, his previous sweet tone replaced by indignation. "What room, what vase are you talking about since I never entered your house, even though I wanted to so much?"

"You never passed through the door of my house? Have you forgotten? Have you forgotten the night we spent together with the vase filled with violets? Have you forgotten our night?"

"I would always bid you farewell outside your door."

"You forgot our night? We left the window open even though the night was chilly, we left it open because we burned with passion and love. You touched me and I lost all my senses. How many times that night did I climb out the window to see the stars, and you joined me."

The audience was now sitting on the edge of their seats, seduced by her words and if they were not curious about what would transpire, they themselves would open the windows and disappear into the night.

"We never spent a night together," the man insisted in vain.

"We spent the whole night making love and when we woke up the next morning, it was raining, a sudden spring shower. I put my hand outside the window to collect water but you complained that you were cold. I had left the window open all night and you caught a cold, so I offered to make you tea with lemon."

Even the light wind that was blowing could not break the silence in the theater as the audience followed the scene with excitement. It wasn't every day that you would come across a love story like this.

"When I returned with the aromatic tea supplemented with nutmeg and honey, you had left. The bed was empty, with the sheets crumpled up on your side of the bed. I dropped the cup to the floor as I ran to catch you, discarding my pride together with the cup. I ran down the stairs and pulled open the door to bring you back. You had turned the corner in the rain and disappeared from sight, I could not see you anywhere."

"So I didn't spend the night with you," the man repeated again, seeking the attention of the audience and the leading lady.

"I was furious, beside myself. I could not stay inside the house, I ran into the rain looking for you. I suddenly found myself in the fields we were yesterday, there where we had picked flowers, exchanging terms of endearment. Some flowers looked at me as if they were mocking me as the rain nurtured them and strengthened them.

'You think you're smart,' I was mad at them and wanted to crush them with my heels. I went from one to the other, none remained upright until I was too tired to destroy any more. I then discovered that, even though it had stopped raining, I was still being drenched with my tears." She lowered her voice and all the flowers in the hall fluttered again in a gusting orgasm.

"I never spent the night with you," the man roared. "We walked up to your door and I left you."

"Are you such a hypocrite to deny our night, our one and only night together? After that night I never went with a man again, I have never loved another man since then. Everyone called me frigid and aloof but I melted only for you. People murmured behind my back that that I had no feelings, that I had never loved, but I had loved you. I spent my whole life remembering that one unique night we spent together and you deny it?"

"Marilena, what are you talking about."

"I have not said a word until now, but I cannot contain myself anymore. As soon as I saw you climbing onto the stage and recognizing me, I just could not hide anymore, pretending that men meant nothing to me, while I had loved you and I still do." He voice now mingled with tears, coming and going ethereally in the theater, but despite the warmth of her voice, the current that was formed became cooler.

"Marilena, I did not stay with you, I did not come to your house, we never slept together!" The man, now aged and tired, blinked his eyes continuously to escape the harshness of the spotlights that focused on him as he looked around for support.

Elvina remained under the spotlight, pushing her hair away from her face in the manner characteristic of Marilena Evangelou, as if it was her own. However, behind her and away from the spotlights, the Theatrical Diva raised her head up high while her mouth opened wide to scream as loud as she could:

"You did stay one night with me!!"

"You're lying, you never had me!" shouted the man, his voice overshadowing hers as he repeated malevolently, "You never had me, not even once!"

Marilena jumped on him to make him stop while the flowers in the audience waved madly, some to the left and some to the right, some towards Marilena and some towards the man. Their movements soon jumbled up and they began to fall apart, torn to pieces, petals with leaves, leaves with stems.

One or two rose fell at Elvina's feet and she bent to pick them up. As she touched them, they colored her hands, turning to blood. She turned her palms under the light and saw they were covered with blood, so she dropped the flowers onto the stage floor, forming blood spatters.

The flowers were then swept away by a strong wind blowing from all sides, falling onto the stage, showering the people there. Wherever they settled, their leaves opened, causing blood to run.

The man's shirt turned red with blood as it dripped down. Marilena fell to the floor and was buried by the flowers that whistled as they settled on her. The wind that was blowing was icy cold, when suddenly a woman's voice was heard above the storm:

"So you loved me? So you were faithful? So you never cheated on me?"

"Eleonora, don't you believe me as well?"

Nikos was Eleonora's husband. Eleonora and Nikos were the couple that had built the pavilion as testimony to their love, surrounded by creepers and lilies.

Elvina did not know anymore what was happening, she didn't know with whom to side with. But Nikos did not give up.

"I never went with another woman, not even with Marilena," he vowed to his wife.

"But you didn't come home one night, I waited for you all night and you appeared the next morning, tired and coughing. Something was wrong with the car was your excuse, you said it suddenly stopped and wouldn't start again, it kept you out all night and I believed you . . ." The woman's voice sounded more desperate than the raging storm. The wind nearly tore the seats from the floor, even though they were screwed tightly. The velvet curtains fluttered back and forth as if made of paper.

Elvina did not know what else to do but crawl into the curtain, the velvet world of her childhood fantasies, until the shadows and the currents calmed down.

However, instead of calming down, Eleonora, Nikos's wife, a tall lean woman wearing her long straight-lined elegant clothes and the bun of her era, stood out in the crowd. The audience spent their time exchanging views and opinions such as:

"What happened that was so bad?" It was only one night and she can't forgive him?"

"I would never have forgiven him!"

"You deserve it when some woman two-times you behind your back."

"I believe Nikos."

"You're a man aren't you so whose side would you take."

"And you're a woman, so you'll side with the woman."

"Which woman however?" another woman's voice was heard.

Eleonora walked to the front row seats, not paying attention to anyone and addressed her husband.

"I never want to see you again," she spat at him. "Don't you dare come to me," there was sadness in her tone mixed with contempt, which made Marilena get up from the floor, possibly thinking about the harm she had done and speak in a manner that from afar seemed theatrical and hypocritical. She would not feel sorry for the rich lady that was the cause for her not enjoying the man of her life.

"Do you think I made this up in my mind? Because I wanted it so much to be my fantasy when Nikos never passed the door-step into my home and into my body?" concluding her words with a melancholic question and a half-mad glaze in her eyes. This hypocrisy or play-acting—whatever it was—enraged the tall woman with the hair bun and she yelled:

"I don't care which door he passed through, I'm completely indifferent. It's enough that he stooped so low and dallied with other women. I don't care what happened, but enough is enough. He will never see me again," and it seemed as if she levitated to the ceiling of the theater that did not impede her as she passed through it, followed by a mass of flowers. Roses, carnations and lilies rose from the floor of the stage where they had laid in blood, became flowers again and followed her, thus emptying the theatre, while a ball was heard rolling down the steps at the entrance.

"They have all gone away," realized Elvina, feeling as if there was no one present in the theater other than the actress who was again transformed into a ball of clothes lying on the floor, Nikos who was tottering towards the exit and Stefanos who remained standing at the end of the stage, not moving while his expression remained unchanged as the tragedy was played out.

"They have all gone," replied Nontas, verifying that which she had realized. "They disappeared in a flash" as he laughed maliciously.

But Marilena stood up erect like a head priest, not giving up. "What did poor me do?" she began to lament. "Nikos, don't leave," running to him. She grabbed him by the shoulders and then by the legs, and was dragged across the floor as she tried to stop him.

"Nikos I love you! I have never stopped loving you. I did everything for you because I loved you. Nikos, it is not too late, I have been waiting for you since the night you took me home and refused to come in."

"So you admit, you malicious hussy, that what you said before was a lie, that you never slept with me?"

"I do not know what I'm saying Nikos. I do not know what happened, my love. My mind is so confused. I see you in my bed, you must have been there and it was not a dream . . ."

"You did all this to take me away from Eleonora, you wicked creature, and you accomplished it. You destroyed a love that endured more than life itself," he cried out as he fell down, his pure white silken hair shaking by his sobbing, pushing Marilena away. "Did you think that you could make me yours with your tricks? You never had me and you never will." He stood up suddenly, strong and erect, held onto his cane and turned his back on her.

"My life is wasted now," Marilena lamented to herself as she lay on the floor. "I squandered my life for you, my whole life has gone down the drain," she cried as she collected dust and flower remnants, rubbing her eyes with her fingers which melted the make-up and eye-shadows she had put on her face for the show. She now looked like a freakish mask that was broken, with a huge eye looking at the exit that sucked Nikos out while a tear, blackened by her mascara, rolled down her face.

Another red eye, puffed up by the anguish she felt, looked desperately at the empty stage, and she did not feel like climbing up again. Her mouth tensed up, the make-up emphasizing her cheeks and her jaw, as if she was a clown. There were no lips however, nor openings in her nose, while there was no inkling of a mouth further down.

Her cross-eyed glance looked left and right for Nikos, but he had left some time ago. As for the stage, it suddenly darkened as Nontas, in charge of general duties, now found the time to turn off the spotlights. Darkness was now everywhere, her fingers moving on the floor, and since there was no mouth to speak, she wanted to complain that the lights on the stage had been turned off prematurely, but the show had ended and there was no reason for them to remain on. She knew this so she lay down and pressed against the floor, becoming one with the dust. Nothing was in the place she was previously.

"Where is Marilena Evangelou?" asked Elvina as she searched for the actress but couldn't find her anywhere. "Marilena!" She yelled out but there was no response, nor did the Theatrical Diva appear.

"Forget her, it'll be some time before we see her again," philosophized Nontas and continued, "We may never see her again . . ."

"Where did she go, what happened?" Elvina couldn't understand what had occurred.

"When people realize that they cannot change events, that they cannot go back, they then calm down and disappear to never appear again," Nontas informed her, choosing his words carefully.

"You're saying that we will never see Marilena Evangelou again and that she will disappear from the garden," Elvina repeated like a puppet.

"Yes" said Nontas quietly.

"I don't know what to believe about her and Nikos," wondered the young girl.

"That's what great loves are all about," said Nontas, sighing heavily.

"That's what great loves are all about," the ambulance driver's words were now repeated by Stefanos.

"Do you also know about great loves?" asked Nontas sarcastically.

"How can he not know," Elvina defended Stefanos. "From what he confided to me, he is one of the few who loved so much and was betrayed."

"Leave it for now, I can't stand any more sentimentalities," snorted the short restless man as he burst out, "I would give anything to have my cruiser!"

"Your cruiser?" wondered Elvina, "It was an ambulance, wasn't it?"

"I nick-named it my cruiser since it had a siren, and when I floored the pedal no one could catch me," he laughed as he looked at the girl slyly, his lips opening in laughter as he exposed his yellow nicotine-stained teeth. "I really miss the bugger," he continued. "One day I was driving my cruiser behind a hospital, which was on duty that day, and we had just dropped off a customer there," showing his teeth as he grinned widely. "My customers included those at death's door and those that were already dead, whatever, we transported them all. Anyway, we dropped him off and went back on duty for the next one. It was a never-ending circle and we did not even have a minute for ourselves.

Anyway, I was driving along the narrow street outside the hospital, cars parked to the left, when I noticed a broad walking on the right side holding a bouquet of flowers in her hand. She was going to visit someone in the hospital. A young girl up to there, wearing tight jeans, and my God, Stefanos, what an ass!" he said to the young man. "It was firm and full-bodied. She wiggled it as she walked on her high-heeled boots, my eyes nearly popped out as I stopped to look at her. How could I take my eyes of her backside and suddenly fate played its hand. I lost control of my vehicle and just managed to turn it before hitting her, crashing into a parked car. Shouting and bedlam followed, the parked car's owner appeared from nowhere, swearing like hell. Cutie stopped to look at the scene, her front was just as good as her behind. I tell you, she was at least two meters tall in all her glory. 'I crashed for your sake,' I whistled at her, 'My eyes were glued on you and how could I unglue them. You have to reward me!'

I asked her even though I was certain it was unattainable, but I asked and she answered:

'I will give you my flowers because the way you drive, you will end up there where they can only bring you flowers,' and she left, leaving the flowers in my hands.

I became the laughing stock of all the curious bystanders watching the accident. The bitch, thinking that I will crash . . . !" He suddenly stopped sadly, putting his hand to his eyes to hide his sorrow.

"I don't think I will come again," Elvina said sadly.

They had reached the gate without realizing it, passing through it in the night that had no moon, with only a few stars shining through the clouds.

"It's going to rain," the girl said shivering.

"I like to hear the rain spattering down," Stefanos spoke after being quiet for quite a while. They were already walking towards the small bench sitting among the microscopic glows of the lanterns that flickered on and off, afraid of the approaching storm, even though they were protected by small glass panes.

"I won't come back," Elvina repeated, but neither of the two men showed that they had heard her. "That's what I'm saying," she murmured in their silence, wondering why they were not in the least interested in stopping her.

"You'll come back. Others have also said they will be leaving us but they couldn't make it," Nontas smiled quietly as he looked conspiratorially at Stefanos.

Chapter 3

THE ACCEPTANCE

Elvina did not have the time to leave the dark garden which despite the silence that enveloped it, was full of questions when various noises were heard coming from the dense vegetation. Somebody was trying to pass through it and who else could it be but the little imp, the bald-headed boy. He was followed by the woman who cared for him and who was pleading with him unsuccessfully to go to bed.

"It is not the time to go running around, let's go so I can tuck you into bed."

"Not without my ball, not without my ball," he retorted as he grabbed Elvina's hemline, almost unraveling it.

"Don't bother the lady," she yelled at him.

"She's not a lady, she's young and I'm not bothering her as she's my friend," stated the small boy, raising his head to stare at Elvina to verify what he was saying. Even though he had released her dress, which was good, he had also at the same time made her heart beat more quickly. A ten-year old boy without hair considered her his friend.

"Of course we are fiends," Elvina announced, "What happened to your ball?"

"He left it at the theater, explained the woman.

"Let's go and get it," requested the youngster.

"It's nighttime . . ." Elvina began to refuse him.

"I don't care, let's go there to get it," the small boy insisted while Elvina caressed his bald head absentmindedly. Suddenly her fingers became entangled in strong hairs that twined themselves around her wrist like tentacles as the small boy dragged her towards the gate of the garden.

"Elvina, where are you going?" Stefanos shouted at her while the woman looked at the small boy who would not listen to her, as he preferred Elvina over her, a new woman who no one knew her background and was supposedly good-hearted as she ran around during the night to look for a ball.

However, Elvina could not see where she was going as she was being dragged by the small boy, so she suddenly ran into the cripple, who was taking his night walk around the pavilion using his short legs.

"Where are you all going?" He stopped walking and stood in front of them, blocking the road. The young girl thought he was cheerful today since he had presented the show: "Excerpts from A Streetcar Named Desire, Act II, Scene III" and "Mother Courage-Brecht, monologue."

He memorized it all, as instructed by the Theatrical Diva, but as he confided to Marilena Evangelou and to Elvina during rehearsals, he wasn't completely green. When he lived a lifetime in an armchair as a cripple, he read theatrical works amongst other things. Nothing escaped him, from newspapers and crossword puzzles to philosophy and history. It could be that he had read some of the works from which excerpts had been interpreted by the actress, and as he confessed, he had read them out aloud.

"I read theatrical works out aloud, changing my voice for the various roles when I was alone and no one could hear me," he added shyly, his eyes downcast. "I would put the script in front of me and act out all the characters, even the female parts, as much as I could of course," and a sweetness shone across his wooden expressionless face as he spoke, while Marilena commented:

"I knew that you were one of us and that is why I chose you to present our show," while Elvina, surprised, murmured:

"I would never be able to spend my whole life trapped in an armchair."

The cripple now grabbed the small boy who was trying to pass him and sat him down next to him on a bench.

"I'm going for my ball, I forgot it at the theater. You can also come with us," the small boy tried to entice him since he could not escape him.

"No one can go to the theater without Marilena or her consent," said the cripple with a severe tone, because, from the time the actress considered him hers, he would protect her and her house, which was her theater.

"I want my ball!" the small boy screeched out and he would have dashed towards the exit if the man had not been holding him tightly.

"You have many balls," the woman/mom tried to calm him down.

"I want that one!!" he screamed.

"You're a spoilt brat, how does your mother tolerate you?" said Nontas crossly while Elvina wavered. She could take him to the theater but she didn't know the address and besides, it would be closed at this time.

She had never gone alone to the rehearsals. She was always accompanied by Marilena and the others. Marilena would open the door and let them in. How Elvina could find someone to unlock the door for them. But before she could finish her thoughts, the small boy, for whom Nontas' words seemed to have sunk in, escaped the clutches of the cripple and began rolling amok on the ground. In between his sobbing and his trepidation, his tufts of hair began falling from his head. Everyone moved away from him, avoiding contact as he howled and thrashed with his hands and feet, digging a hole in the ground.

"I'm not spoilt, my mom never spoilt me, my mom is the best mom in the world. How could she spoil me?" he shouted, words and tears spilling out of his mouth, together with pieces of broken toys that included miniature metallic cars, plastic guns and telephones, broken and bitten. "I broke and destroyed my toys and then bit them before spitting them into my plate." He got up from the ground showing a deformed puffed-up blue face from which pieces of flesh fell out.

Elvina started shivering again. She could see his teeth, seemingly huge, in the lower law of his mouth, which had only an upper lip, and he suddenly spewed out fluids.

"They would insert the serum into my elbow. What went into me from there I would throw out from here," pointing with his finger to the hole in his mouth, proud that he could accomplish this. "They said that this serum would keep me alive but I ejected it through my mouth," pointing now to the saliva dribbling out of his mouth, mixed with pieces of flesh, fruit juices and milk. "Imagine serum, serum with drugs and vitamins. Mom, bring me some fried chips. Yes, she brought me whatever I asked for, is that why I'm spoilt?"

With the help of the woman/mom he began to wipe the tears and vomit from his face and body. "I wouldn't ask for whatever came to my mind if I wasn't sick . . ." he whined.

"But you used to break your toys even when you were not sick, how could your mother stand you?" The cripple repeated Nontas' words in his loud overbearing voice, putting the small boy in his place. The latter then began to tremble.

"Do you think that's why I became sick, because I was a bad boy?" he asked unhappily, ready to punish whatever had remained of his body, without being able to find some comfort in his doubtfulness and his misery.

"Tell me, tell me!" he addressed the cripple as well as the others with his look, which was the only human part that had remained in him. His complete body and half his face was now a formless mass.

Elvina was still panic-stricken, how could the boy that had held her by her dress become like this?

"So that's what worrying you", Nontas now spoke more tenderly as he hugged the small boy. "Do you know how many bad children grow up completely healthy? Every one of them, I guarantee it and besides, you weren't a bad boy, I know you well. I promise you you're not a bad boy. It was unfortunate you became sick. You were the zero point something percent statistically of children who become seriously sick. Listen to me, I know these things." He did not stop hugging the small boy and caressing him and holding him against him.

"Are you telling me the truth?" the small boy managed to whisper while gradually regaining his human form as Nontas spoke to him. "Is he telling the truth?" he asked the woman/mom and Elvina, looking at both of them in expectation.

"If all the really bad children became sick and died before they grow up, the world would be a paradise," said the cripple vociferantly.

"What did he say?" said the small boy in a frightened tone, as he was too mixed up to understand the meaning. "I'm to blame for my sickness, if I did not worry my mom so much I'd be healthy now," he began to cry again.

"Listen to me!" the cripple caught his attention with his bass voice. "You're not a bad boy, but neither was I when I was born paralyzed from the waist down. I was born paralyzed even before I had the opportunity to be a bad or a good boy. My fate was to enter the world deficiently, that's life." His argument seemed to convince the small boy, who continued insistently:

"You telling the truth? You were born like that?" a small ray of hope seemed to enter his ravaged face, "You were really born like that?" he repeated his phrase hoping his mind would accept it. "So I was fated to become sick," he concluded and seemed to become more alive. His eyes opened wide as he looked happily at those around him.

"Yes!" said the man steadily.

"It's exactly that my little friend, didn't I say so," Nontas said, endorsing the cripple while still hugging the small boy.

"It's the truth!" said the woman/mom as she took him into her arms to mollycoddle him.

"How could you think you were to blame for your sickness?" wondered Elvina as she smiled at him.

"That's why the little imp couldn't keep quiet and nearly drove us all mad," Nontas concluded as he supposedly scolded the small boy, who now stood up and seemed to grow taller as he whispered softly, and only Elvina, who was standing next to him, heard him.

"My mom loved me. Whatever I did to her, she still loved me. And me, I worried because I was a bad boy and then a sick boy tormenting her but it wasn't my fault." He finished speaking without wondering any more as he looked around at the darkness that covered them all.

The light from the lanterns just managed to illuminate a small circle around each tree, with each overlapping circle catching the gaze of the small boy. Circles that seemed to pull on him as if they were tied to him. They seemingly enticed him to start walking, the others just staring at him without trying to stop him as he walked away mechanically, leaving behind him a small mist.

"Where's he going?" asked a shaken Elvina.

"To his grave" replied Nontas softly and solemnly, with an expression she had never seen before.

"Won't we see him again?" complained the woman/mom.

"He will never leave his grave," explained the cripple to Elvina.

"We've lost the little rascal," agreed Nontas.

"But what happened?" asked Elvina, not understanding as a cold sweat drenched her body.

"The small lad died from his sickness some time ago," began Stefanos, who had been silent up to now, "However . . ." Elvina cut him off:

"He had died? He is dead?" she whispered, trembling uncontrollably. What was this she was hearing, but it would be a lie to say that this was not completely unexpected. Many curious and unexplained things had occurred metaphysically in her association with the permanent and transient frequenters of the garden, but she had not let her mind ask why. She never asked herself why she saw the small boy sometimes with hair and sometimes complete bald whenever he appeared before her with a decomposed look, and also why did he complain that he never grew older.

But what was she doing here with them and why didn't she just run for it? Her legs remained motionless as if buried in the ground, unable to transport her, and it seemed to be Stefanos' words that imposed her intentions and her mobility.

"The sickness beat him. Instead of growing up he died. He's dead but was being tormented, he just could not rest in peace in his grave so he appeared every day until he could find his peacefulness," Stefanos spoke slowly and steadily as if reading a memorized text.

"We don't come out of our graves again when we make peace with ourselves," the cripple was dogmatic and absolute as he explained the disappearance of the small boy.

"The same thing happened with the Theatrical Diva, we've lost her as well," reminded Nontas. "She tried so hard to make Nikos hers, even up to the last moment, but just couldn't manage it, so she's now peaceful forever."

"Was she also dead?" asked Elvina wearily. Yes, the actress who she met was dead, that was why she complained that she would be walking around for centuries in an aged condition because she had died at an advanced age. She was dead and that was why she suddenly disappeared from their sight, sinking into the floor of the stage while Elvina was still looking for her.

"And she'll never return, so forget about her," Stefanos' voice resembled an injection that hurt as it was inserting anesthesia into the vein.

Elvina could not react to such disclosures that explained some of her doubts, but at the same time puzzled her, while allowing herself to be appeased by the effects exerted on her by the young man. Enough for today, she did not want to hear any more but Nontas continued to blabber on in his usual manner.

"Only we have remained for the time being, but others will come, so many funerals are taking place. We are never wanting for people; new people, new stories," Nontas chuckled while the cripple shifted his legs before beginning his snippety-hop walk without showing any interest in continuing the conversation. "Some of them have been ghosts for years now outside their graves," he continued while emitting an extra loud laugh that resembled an outcry.

"Some blame themselves, others delay as they wait to meet their loved ones . . ." the woman/mom ended her unfinished phrase as she tried to justify various behaviors, saddened at the loss of the small boy. But there are still quite a few children in the garden that needed looking after.

"Others just don't know what's happening to them," said Nontas, continuing the conversation, maligning softly so that only Elvina would hear him. "Let's say, Stefanos for instance,"

"What going on with Stefanos?" Elvina wanted to know.

"The young one has taken the bait," the former ambulance driver winked at the woman/mom. But before anyone could continue the matter, the balls of the small boy started rolling towards them one by one from the row of trees and pathway that had swallowed him up. The first one was his soccer ball followed by a basket ball, then a second soccer ball, a multi-colored beach-ball and a ping pong ball which hit the stones, giving off a terrifying sound that frightened Elvina, while Stefanos, Nontas, the cripple and the woman/mom scurried around picking up the balls.

"He's left them for us since he doesn't need them anymore," smiled the woman/mom sadly. "I will give then to the other children to play with!" she shouted happily as she would then be able to connect with them.

The hours they spent talking soon passed and the lanterns began to lose their illumination as dawn approached. Nontas kicked the large soccer ball towards the church.

"You'll break something," Elvina shouted at him as she ran behind the ball and kicked it towards the woman/mom while the short ambulance driver disappeared into the rich vegetation. The young girl wanted to help the woman carry all the balls since Stefanos had disappeared, probably so as not to continue the revelations. At any event, the children would soon be waking up and would charge down there, and of course they would never say no to an extra ball.

All that could be heard for some time now was the sound of the balls bouncing against the stone paving of the pathway and the marble monuments. Everyone, young and old, played with them, throwing them or kicking them from one side to the other until they ended up in the hands of the children and the adults who were playing soccer next to the pavilion. Stefanos was with them, playing from dawn to dusk.

There were some days, sometimes even the following day, when time passed peculiarly for Elvina, since the days were a vacuum except for some periods that were filled with specific images, such as the images of the rain that today was either pelting down or coming down in a fine mist and yesterday or a little while ago it was not raining. And since it was raining they would not be playing, thought Elvina logically as she looked for Stefanos.

"Are they playing? Continuously, without stopping," Nontas informed her.

"But it's raining," she said indignantly.

"So what, a little rain won't harm them," laughed the short thin man jeeringly.

"It doesn't bother me as well." Elvina realized then that her bones were not aching despite the humidity and the rain, nor was her breathing labored.

"Come here," Nontas took her with him to sit under one of the monuments that protected them from the cascading rain. "Dear Sir, aren't we acceptable?" he continued, inviting in this manner a passing shadow that turned around and regained a face and body, the face of a well-known television presenter wearing a well-cut suit.

"Are you talking to me?" his cultured voice sounded surprised that someone like Nontas sought his company, but his eyes then strayed to Elvina, whose wet hair shone even more than black crystal while her skin resembled a mirror.

"How long have you been here?" he kept staring at her.

"I don't know." Elvina felt his admiration for her increasing and her mirror/skin reflected the blushing she felt, formed by his gaze. This was why she could only reply with a simple "I don't know." Besides, she really didn't know.

"Who are you?"

"The prettiest girl that has passed by here," replied Nontas as he introduced them to each other. "Of course you recognized him", and continued, "The young girl would like to ask you something."

"Ask him what? I'm looking for Stefanos," she answered, confused.

"This does concern Stefanos," explained Nontas. "Since you are a journalist and a famous one, with reporting skills and the right information, tell us, did you happen to hear about a double murder carried out about six months ago, followed by a suicide".

Elvina was stunned. If Stefanos had managed to kill himself with the last bullet that passed through him, he had lied to her that he had missed and had not killed himself and that the police were after him, and that was why he was hiding in the garden. It was a lie so as not to frighten her. He was dead, just like the small bald-headed boy and Marilena Evangelou, as were all the other permanent and transient visitors spending their time in the park.

They were not just unemployed or pensioners or visitors, they were people who had passed into another world, far away and unknown, she knew it. The cripple who could finally walk was dead, the drunkard who had driven off the cliff in his drunken state, Eleonora and Nikos, the hordes of people who had filled the theater and then disappeared like the wind.

After her initial shock, Elvina found she was not surprised or insane. She knew that there was no other explanation for the silent presences that dematerialized in the wind. She could hear it now being said and discussed. She managed to pull herself together to hear the journalist's reply, which was an indirect verification that all those who were around her were not alive.

"If a double homicide and a suicide took place six months before I came here?"

Here? Here where? In the world where the dead wandered around, rationalized Elvina. The clarification sought by the TV presenter was whether this was an event that took place before his death, with his thoughts giving him a sullen expression that seemingly took away all his charm.

"Of course before you came here," clarified Nontas.

"Nothing happened. I would have read about it in the newspapers, I would have followed it on television. It's impossible for me not to know." The cripple jumped out of nowhere, standing in front of them on his stubby feet, as he paused in his stroll.

"Specifically, a man shot and killed his girlfriend who was cheating on him with his best friend. He killed the woman first and then the friend who had stolen her away from him, and he then committed suicide!" Nontas added a final exclamation mark to his description of the crimes.

"No triple homicide occurred," the journalist was categorical and turned to Elvina, ignoring Nontas. "How did a gorgeous girl like you get involved with crimes?" and as he looked at her, his face reformed again. But this second expression of his froze Elvina instead of warming her up as before.

"There's someone who says that he did it for the sake of love," she spoke quietly and melodiously, as if she could not believe her words but was just announcing the news.

"Impossible! This would not have escaped my attention," the journalist was definite.

"Nor me," confirmed the cripple. "I would read every single line in the newspapers since I spent all my time sitting in an armchair." He finished his phrase and turned to continue his walkabout.

"He lied to me," Elvina was flabbergasted.

"He lied to us," corrected Nontas.

"Why should he tell such a hideous lie?" the young girl was dumbfounded while the journalist tried unsuccessfully to attract her attention. He finally just grabbed her hand.

"Don't touch me!" she yelled looking at him, long tangled hair, long nails yellow-stained from nicotine, as he grabbed her wrist, while mud dripped from the corners of his eyes. "Leave me alone!" as she pushed him away and began to run, run far away from all these damned people who were pulling her into their world.

There were times when Elvina lied to her parents and to her friends. The second lie was made to give credence to the first, the third to give foundation to the previous two, the next to save all that preceded, and so on, and everyone believed her. No one doubted her when she put her mind to trick them.

"I spent ten days in August with my parents on the island," she would say to her boyfriend at that time. She was of course not with her parents on the island, she was instead tucked away in the coolness of her apartment chilling with her green plants. She had better things to do than run after him looking for an empty umbrella on the Attica beaches filled with hot sweaty bodies covered in suntan oil.

Besides, she was playing the role of an up-and-coming actress, "This year a small role in the theater and next year, who knows." She would then lower her eyes modestly, showing her shadowed eyelids. "Which theater should I select to buy tickets for my friends so as to fill the hall?" with the recipient of her fairytales showing much enthusiasm. "What a pity the show has just finished its run. If I had met you earlier I would have had my own claque."

"Where will I then see you?" he insisted, deluded that he was going out with someone famous.

"First row at your bed," she would say, to get rid of him as well as to turn him on, even though she rarely acted on these words. She would leave him to go on tour and would call him as soon as she returned, but in fact she would nestle in her apartment away from everyone and everything. Why did she tell so many lies? she wondered.

"Why did you lie to me?" she asked Stefanos, who then scowled and turned red-faced up to his ears, just like a howling baby.

"Everyone lies", he defended himself.

"I have also told many lies," she admitted, "but not as bad as yours," she clarified softly.

"Would it have been better if I was a murderer rather than a liar who you exposed?" he complained.

Nontas, the cripple, the woman/mom who had still not replaced the small bald-headed boy with someone else to care for, and the journalist who—after thinking about it—was now curious to find out what was going on, all crept behind the bushes and the monuments to eavesdrop.

As Stefanos turned towards Elvina, he started sobbing, falling devastated onto the bench, while seemingly holding a photograph.

It's strange thought the young girl, when she had met him for the first time his face was as motionless as a photograph.

"I don't want to look at my useless mug any more, I'll throw it away," his outburst was directed at the picture-frame while his features hardly resembled it anymore. It was a mass of soft haggard flesh sprouting wild black sparse hairs that formed a beard. He frightened Elvina as this was the first time he had appeared like this before her.

"Look up," said Nontas, pull her by the elbow. There was nothing high up, no rain, no sun, no clouds, just an empty colorless sky.

"No woman wanted me the way I was, empty and colorless," Stefanos now sounded desperate as he followed the movement of her head and her gazing at the sky. Happily he now resembled the sad-looking boy in the photograph. "No woman loved me," said the young man, now holding the photograph in his hand, ready to either throw it away or place it back into his memory. "The first girl that I asked out sat in the school-desk next to me and she said yes when I asked her to go to the movies with me," his voice betraying the enthusiasm that the success had caused at that time.

"Tell us, tell us!!" The audience was ready for a tear-jerking story.

"She never came," he immediately disappointed them. "I arrived first, bought two tickets and waited at the entrance of the cinema. We lost the good seats as she was late. I wondered whether she sat in the front rows, in the middle ones or upstairs where I usually went. I never found out as she did not come.

The next day at school I asked what happened and why she stood me up. When did I stand you up, she replied, looking at me in a supposedly curious manner but full of irony. She then continued on, saying how could she have said yes, she would go to the movies with me when she had already arranged to go to the cafeteria with her friends. So I never ever invited a girl to go to the movies with me, and of course a long time passed before I again went . . ."

Nontas laughed but Elvina felt sad as Stefanos continued:

"And she wasn't the only one. No one ever loved me, I never stood out anywhere. I wasn't something special so why should women want me?" He felt sad as his hands suddenly broke the glass pane of the photograph, cutting his finger in the process. But it didn't seem to hurt and he wasn't bothered with the blood dribbling over his palms. "I should have started killing when she first started acting smart with me so I could have dressed her in blood," his voice deepened and he went wild, raising his hands to rub the blood all over his face.

"Killing is in my blood even though I never actually went through with it," he growled like a wounded animal and made an effort to continue. "It took a long time for me to again ask a woman for a date, I did it after the army when I was working. To hell with it, I told myself, everyone's going out with some woman and they're no better than me, so why can't I do it? Some responded while others did not. The last instance was with a girl who worked in the computer department of the company where I was an accountant."

"You told me something different . . ." Elvina cut him off softly as she remembered his stories about expensive cars and bars in Athens and in foreign capitals. "You really told me a pack of lies."

"Only you? All of us!" Nontas said, nodding his head.

"It was my myth. Now it's gone, you took it away from me. I really enjoyed telling everyone I was rich with cars, yachts and women, lots of women, none could resist my charm and my money. I never had anything, nor did I have any woman. Are you happy now? Nothing, no riches, no cars, no girls, not even any blood. When I cut my finger with the piece of glass, no blood came out."

It was strange that all the previous loss of blood had disappeared, so his appearance showed no blemishes: clean face, clean clothes and no signs of blood, even though slivers of glass had pierced the flesh of his fingers.

"Dead people don't bleed," explained the cripple.

"I know, I'm an expert in these things," confirmed Nontas.

"Forget the glass," Elvina urged Stefanos. She took the photograph and glass shards from his hands and tried to stick them together again. The pieces of glass joined together like a jigsaw puzzle and the photograph was soon whole again.

"Whatever happened to the girl from the computer department?" she wanted to know since she loved listening to or watching sentimental films at the cinema or on television, especially those without a happy ending. But she couldn't know the ending without first watching almost to the last scene of the movie, and when the happy ending was definite she would leave the cinema mad as hell or just change channels on television.

"You're overdoing it," her girlfriend Natalia said indignantly, as did Sonia her roommate. Both were driven mad by the tall muscular man with the strong chin and mythical wealth who finally marries the girl in a spectacular scene on a sun-drenched island wearing endless meters of tulle. "Just because you fucked up you can't bear seeing people continuing their lives on the tube or on the screen."

However, she was certain that from what he has said to date, the story of Stefanos would not have a happy ending, and that was why she wanted to learn more about the girl in the computer department.

He sighed, "What happened with Lina? Same as the others that preceded her, nothing scintillating. We were going out, seeing each other . . ."

"Didn't she used to stand you up on your dates?" Nontas' tone was both teasing and friendly.

"That wasn't the problem," Stefanos replied, "She was perfect with respect to time and place, the essentials were missing. 'I love you, I love you' I would shout. I would repeat it as I kissed her and hugged her to me. 'I love you' I would whisper into her ear, 'Do you love me? Say it, let me hear you saying it, talk to me, tell me you want me,' I didn't stop for one second as I touched her, my fingers caressing her breast but no further. This wasn't magical, unreachable, indefinable that drove you crazy. The only thing I felt was the need for sex which would disappear in seconds.

Afterwards I didn't give a damn whether I would meet her again or not or whether I made love to her or with anyone else. At first my heart throbbed somewhat . . . Will she call me when she saw my no reply message? Will she let me kiss her? And when I did kiss her, it was nothing to write home about. Her mouth tasted of lemon from the sorbet she had eaten earlier, so she smelt nice, I wondered if I tried for second base would she let me?

She did let me on the third attempt but no sparks. I think she felt the same way about me; she seemed to tolerate me so she could say she was involved in a relationship, that there was a man who called her on the phone. In fact my calls to her were scheduled: at eleven in the morning to say 'Good morning', at two to arrange when we would meet, nothing in-between.

She never called me even once, only once or twice but not to say that she wanted me or that she wanted to see me or that she missed me, she wanted to ask something stupid like what was the name of the movie we had seen, if X cell-phone company had cheaper programs than Y company, what cell model should her friend buy.

That was the level of our relationship at a time when I thirsted for a love that would arouse me, a love like that between Eleonora and Nikos, a desperate love story like Marilena's that even death could not shatter.

That was the kind of love I wanted to experience, a love that would make me shiver for her, make me lose my words over her, make me want to compose a song for her.

I didn't care about money or cars. I just wanted to love somebody . . . to fall in love." He then fell off the bench onto the ground, which slowly-slowly sucked him in until nothing was left of Stefanos except the photograph, standing upright, looking at them with motionless eyes.

A printed piece of paper behind a piece of glass was all that was left for a shocked Elvina to look at.

"Nice photograph. Stefanos was a handsome boy."

"I can't deny that," agreed Nontas, "but mark my words, we haven't finished with him yet."

"What do you mean?" the young girl asked him.

"Who knows how many more years he will be bugging us until he finds the love he is looking for, if ever," as he turned his back on them.

Elvina sat on a bench looking at the photograph of the young man while the journalist who had been looking for an opportunity to catch her alone, now took advantage of the opportunity that had arisen.

"I know a little in-place near here that is just sumptuous. Have you ever been to the hotel "Grande Bretagne?" he asked condescendingly.

"He took me to Prague," she whispered wistfully as she continued looking at the photograph, ignoring the man who was talking to her.

"He was just a small-time hustler who filled you with lies, stories about imaginary homicides, trips abroad, sports cars, and whatever else he could imagine in order to win you over," the big-shot said angrily.

"Is that why he did it, to make a pass at me?" Elvina looked at him in amazement, "It never entered my mind," she continued wide-eyed, "He's dead . . ."

"My girl, you just don't know what's happening to you," the renowned journalist said angrily, "I don't know why I'm bothering with you," he was mad at himself as he slowly transformed into a shadow under the midday sun that was at that time shining brightly.

"Why is he so mad at me? Why is he saying that I don't know what's happening to me?"

"Ignore him," the woman/mom said trying to comfort her in a tone that sounded unnatural and false, but why? Elvina just could not explain it. "He really thinks he's the cat's whiskers, you're right in giving him the cold shoulder," the woman continued on, drawing her attention from her previous words. "Like hell you would have followed him. What do you and him have in common?"

"Nothing!" Stefanos' voice was heard as he gradually appeared before them. "I am not a fraud," he assured her, "and if I did lie, I lied to myself and no one else. It just happened that you-all also heard it. I just wanted me to hear it as it sounded so nice to my ears. I believed that I had been a rich kid with sports cars and women that threw themselves at my feet. I would leave one and take the other until I met the woman of my dreams. I then gave my all to her, I wanted her to be mine forever. I would have followed her even here and yes, I did it . . . I killed her and was killed so we can be together."

"Stefanos, you've started again," said Elvina, cutting him off as she absentmindedly touched the glass pane of the photograph.

"Does it matter?" he asked shyly, like a little boy who was mischievous. "Does it matter if I tell you whatever comes to mind?"

"No," said Elvina, "Say whatever you want, it doesn't bother me," as she continued touching the glass that covered the photograph, which she now discovered was hot and steamy, like a sweaty forehead, but this was probably due to the sun beating down on them.

If Stefanos was not dead, things would have been different, but Elvina was in general confused. I don't know what's happening to me, she thought, blaming herself, so she decided to run as fast as she could away from Stefanos, even as she wondered why was she running away? What's wrong with me wanting to suddenly run away as if I'm being chased, she asked herself?

But as she looked back, she discovered that tall levitating black shadows seemed to be following her, soundless words flowing from their mouths but she could still hear them echoing insistently in her ears.

"Where are you going? You're the same as us, you can't leave us." They were just about to catch her, they would be passing over her, they were going to trample her. The voices were now augmented by mocking cries and laughter as the figures moved to block the exit.

She remembered when she was young she used to hide under the blankets, and she still continued to do this even now. Whenever she faced difficulties or problems, she would jump under the blankets with her head touching her chest—a loose ball well-hidden under the bedcovers.

"How can you breathe like that, you'll suffocate!" her mother would come and uncover her.

"I'm breathing my own warm air," she would reply and snuggle in more deeply.

Later, Kostas used to yell at her for the same reason and she would reply that she was diving into her blankets.

She now ran to hide from the black scowling shadows that were chasing her, which was now her bed where she was staying, she couldn't remember which way to go so she started to panic. Her feet remained motionless instead of running, they weren't going anywhere. Where was the gate, she couldn't see it, she probably lost the road as she didn't follow the right road in her haste and fear to run away, and she ended up going in another direction.

"Where are you running to?" she was stopped by the cripple who was walking parallel to the fence.

"Let me go!" she tried to avoid him but his hands grabbed her.

"Where do you want to go?" His voice was soft and full of interest in contrast to his hands.

"I want to get away from here so take your hands off me," she screamed in confusion. Where did she get the idea to walk around this haunted place, which would now not let her leave?

"Don't you understand, you're now one of us?" cried a bass voice trying to persuade her.

"What do you mean? I want to go home," she cried as she struggled with him, but it was futile since she was slender and weak. She couldn't get away from him as he still held her, until Stefanos arrived on the scene and saved her from his grappling hands.

"Where were you?" she complained to him as she fell into his arms to get away, without caring that he was also one of the dead. "You left me alone and everyone is trying to drive me crazy."

"My relatives have arrived, they held a memorial service," said Stefanos, explaining his tardiness. "I sat with my mother. She is now so weak and old. She was the first to arrive, washing and polishing the marble slab and the cross and dusting the photograph. She placed new flowers into the vase and began to burn incense . . ."

"So that's why you smell of incense," Elvina discovered and unconsciously pulled away.

"The other relatives and the priest arrived later," the young man continued, pretending that he did not notice her pulling away from him. "I can't stand these rituals but I still remained with my mother. She's turned white and wrinkled in only a few months or it may be the black clothes that make her look ugly."

"It's these as well, but it's mainly because she lost you," Nontas retorted as he suddenly appeared before them. His attention was drawn to the group of mourners who were walking slowly down the road with bowed heads. "Are these your people?" he asked curiously as he glanced at them.

"Yes," confirmed Stefanos in a neutral voice.

"My boy, you're skint as well, you who played the big-shot," Nontas cackled as he watched the faces and figures of the relatives.

"Was I wrong in doing it," laughed Stefanos bitterly as he continued, "I grew up in a ground-floor three-roomed apartment in Patisia. I slept in the living-room with my brother since there was no room elsewhere. Every morning we would fold the sheets and beds and open them up every night. So it was a living-room during the day and a bedroom at night. Elvina, there's my mother," pointing to a black-veiled woman.

Before Elvira could recover from all that which had just occurred, she was again overwhelmed by the presence of Stefanos' relatives and that which was said.

"We ate in the kitchen," the young man continued describing his life. "I was never one for food, I would eat a couple of spoonfuls and then leave the table. I made my mother worry over me my whole life and now I gave her the greatest grief of all. Eat so you can grow tall, she would beg me, eat to be strong. I did the opposite, a couple of mouthfuls and I was out the door."

"Where would you find the appetite for food, since you're in over your head," Nontas reproached him affectionately.

"I didn't expect much," the young man replied melancholically.

"No, you don't expect much," Nontas repeated sarcastically. "No one expects too much but asks for everything, but we all finally end up here," showing off his large yellow-stained bad teeth as a powerfully bad odor emanated from his body, forcing Elvina to move back. She even saw him momentary as a skull, bones without flesh or eyes, with just two jaws with huge teeth that opened and closed to form words and grimaces.

But before she could really feel frightened, the ugly image disappeared as Nontas turned to Stefanos.

"Was your stomach the reason for coming here?" Curiosity was killing the former ambulance driver as the myth surrounding the murders and the violence existed no more.

"No, my stomach was not the cause, my stomach was fine," his lips formed a saddened smile, similar to the photograph. "I don't know what happened to me," his sorrow deepened, his lips taking on a dark eggplant color, "Just as I don't know much about love."

The sorrowfulness spilled out from his lips, darkening his whole face. "I died of an aneurism. That's what I heard the doctor telling my mother who didn't know what had happened to me, she lost me in less than two hours. I felt a terrible pain in my head that made me want to bang it against the wall to relieve the pain, but I didn't do it as I fainted, and that was that."

His head continued to darken as he spoke, making Elvina realize that it was not the sadness that colored his face, it was the blood that had flooded his brain from the aneurism which finally killed him. But she was not the only one who had noticed this because the cripple's voice was heard above the hubbub.

"Stefanos, what happened and you've turned blue? Did a ball hit you on the head?"

This matter of the ball being the cause of Stefanos' color helped to raise the spirits of all three of them, Elvina, Stefanos and Nontas, with a smile breaking out on their mouths. This helped to lighten their bad mood and the gruesome conversation.

"If someone hit you, I'll rearrange his face," threatened the cripple, raising his fists to the air.

"Shut-up," chided Stefanos as the last relatives passed by them. "Talk softer as they may hear us," he admonished him with his hands.

"We'll spoil the ceremony," mocked Nontas.

"I can't stand this smell," the incense pressing on them was as heavy as a tombstone, "Let's go to the seaside to blow off some steam," Stefanos proposed suddenly.

"But isn't the sea far from here?" was Elvina's first reaction.

"When were you ever scared of walking?" retorted Stefanos, who was familiar with her rambles.

"But isn't it cold, it's winter?" was her second thought as she remembered the coats, socks and heavy shoes worn by the relatives who had just passed by them. Even though she was wearing only her silk dress, she wore no stockings and was not cold at all.

"Come on, the water will be warm," Stefanos was already walking briskly and enthusiastically, like a little boy, while Elvina would have gone just to get away from there.

Nontas said discreetly that he would leave them alone, taking the cripple with him.

So the two of them found themselves at the beach in a very short time, short for Elvina's standards.

"I can't go in with such waves," she found herself disappointed as soon as they arrived there. The sea was colored the grey hues of a cloudy winter afternoon as the huge waves smashed their foamy faces onto the shore.

"Follow me," the young man ordered as he dragged her by the hand. Elvina thought that the drops of water from the breaking waves would destroy her dress, but it was already too late. The waves crashed onto her, dragging her back into the deep waters. The water was warm and playful and Elvina now found she was enjoying it.

One moment she was above the waves, the next under it, but she was a good swimmer as she had grown up on an island. Sure she didn't usually enter the sea in such weather, but it wasn't as if she couldn't control it.

Stefanos swam up and down the crests of the sea shouting out in delight.

"This is really something!" Stefanos' words could be heard above the roar of the waves.

"It's great!" she agreed.

They grabbed each other by the hand and dived under the waves. The water near the bottom was quieter and they swam for quite a while before rising to the surface.

"I've never dived this long," she patted herself on the back. "How did I manage to hold my breath for so long?" She swam on her back along the crest of the water to catch her breath.

"It was only for a few seconds," Stefanos contradicted the calculation of her time. Elvina did not persist even though she thought she had spent quite some time underwater.

They now floated on their backs on the waves, like a rider on a horse.

"Mummy, Mummy, look they're swimming in the sea," their serenity was shattered by the voice of a little girl holding her mother's hand as they walked along the pavement next to the beach.

"I don't see anyone." Mother and daughter stood looking out at the sea as the wind blew their hair in all directions.

"Right in front of us Mommy . . . a man and a woman. She's not wearing a bathing suit, she's swimming in a white dress." The little girl pointed at them as Elvina raised her hand to wave and yell 'Hi' at them, loud enough to be heard above the waves.

"Where are they? I can't see anyone," the mother repeated as she searched among the waves.

"Down there, she's waving at us," she turned her mother's head towards the young girl swimming in the sea, while also waving back at her.

"How can they swim in such weather? It's impossible, you don't know what you're saying," after looking for the swimmers, the mother was now doubting her daughter.

"There are two of them . . . a man and a woman. They are now hidden by the waves, they'll soon appear again," the small girl was certain, and sure enough they appeared on the surface of the water.

"I don't see anything," the mother replied after searching the sea again. "No one is swimming in the sea and how could they? It's winter, it's cold and it's blowing. As for you, I just don't know what's got into you and you're acting this way."

"But I can see them!" The small girl was beside herself with anger. "A man and a woman, down there," she stopped and again pointed in the direction where she had last seen them.

"Let's go before I get really mad. There's no one in the sea," the mother was now angry as she pulled her daughter to leave. At the same time an icy chill ran down Elvina's spine and she trembled in response.

"I'm getting cold, let's go," she addressed Stefanos. He seemed indifferent to the incident with the small girl on the pavement.

The next day, it was surely tomorrow, Elvina managed to work it out from the continuation of the bad weather, which was now really bad. It was icy cold in the park but no one felt cold. Nor did she feel the cold, walking around in her silk clothes, which were not affected in the least by the swim in the sea. When they had dried out, her clothes were just as before—starched and clean.

"It's going to snow", Nontas the know-it-all predicted. "Once when it snowed heavily we had to search for our graves," his cackling echoing painfully in Elvina's ears.

"It's not a lie," the bass voice of the cripple attested to the event. "The snow covered the tombstones, only the crosses stuck out. If more snow had fallen, it would have covered them as well and no one would have known if they were in a cemetery or not . . ." he continued, leaving his phrase unfinished.

"It never snows so much in our country," Stefanos added melancholically, "and how long would it have lasted, a couple of days and then what?" He left this unanswered, which allowed Nontas to continue pugnaciously.

"Would we have been resurrected with our graves hidden?"

"Of course not," replied the cripple seriously. "The opposite in fact. The snow reminds me of a huge icy shroud," and he began his narration: "When it snowed I would push my armchair to the window." This was the reason why his arms were so powerful, thought Elvina as he continued. "I sat by the window and watched it falling. It was times like this when I panicked as I thought, I'm paralyzed from the waist down and unable to move, so what would happen if I lost the use of my arms. I thought that the paralysis would gradually creep up to my neck and my head. It would immobilize my whole body, as well as my speech, my hearing, my feeling and even my sight. As time passed I was more worried about the worst happening. I trembled at the thought I would lose my eyesight.

At times like this the snow resembled a shroud and I thought, what would I need my eyesight for, just to see the shroud. I then closed my eyes and remained still, completely still to overcome my fears, but I immediately felt a cold sweat covering my body. I could be blind when I opened my eyes again, and maybe when I tried to move my arms, they would not budge. Do you think I might not hear anything when sometimes the house was completely silent?

On a day like this I cried out, just as my mother was coming in. This scared her and she collapsed, and never recovered. The stroke that I cause her to suffer affected her brain. She would wonder who I was. She never recognized me when she was discharged from the hospital. This wasn't so terrible as she was able with one stroke to be free of me and my misery."

At this point the lips of the cripple turned up ironically. "I then went from bad to worse," he continued. "The nightmares that I would lose whatever remained of my mobility and my contact with my surroundings appeared more and more often. I was too scared to go to bed because as soon as I closed my eyes, the perils would appear. 'You are suffering from myasthenia,' shadows with hoods, pointed hats and noses would murmur behind my back. 'You will never open your eyelids again. We will keep them open with adhesive tape. Look, they're drooping, ready to close unless I use clips. You won't be able to see anything and as for getting out of bed, forget it. You won't have arms to help you hold yourself.'"

As the words came out all jumbled up and tormented from his mouth, the cripple raised his arms and crossed them on his shoulders to prove to himself that he still had them and controlled them.

"This nightmare finally killed me. One night my mouth would not close as my panic increased. The blood then clotted and a thrombus finished me off. But there are still times when I feel that I cannot move, that my limbs are pieces that somebody screwed to my body and that they do not belong to me, that they will desert me and I will again be paralyzed. The thought that I will not have them eats me up day and night, and this is why I'm moving around all the time, making sure that I can still move around.

But now I seem to be stiffening up, I can't move my arms, they are stuck to my body. Will someone please free me, I beg you!"

Stefanos was the first to reach the cripple and pull his arms open while pushing him slightly. The cripple rocked on his feet until he regained his balance, opening and closing his arms at the same time.

"Thanks Stefanos," he muttered quickly and absentmindedly as his mind was focused on beginning his walk again.

"He will never be at peace with himself," the former ambulance driver diagnosed behind his back.

"Imagine spending your whole life trapped in a wheelchair. I couldn't stand this suffering," Elvina defended him, even though he was always offensive with her.

"Everyone has his own burden to carry," philosophized Nontas, sighing heavily in the process. "How I miss my little truck, turning on the siren and stamping on the gas while I zigzag through the traffic. 'Move out of the way, Nontas is coming through' I yelled at them as I looked at them presumptuously through my window or in my mirrors. 'I will crush you, dudes, if you don't get out of my way.'"

"In any event, you never raced to get your patients to the hospital on time. You didn't give a damn about them, you just loved to drive at high speed," Stefanos interrupted him sourly.

"You can't do this job if you don't like to drive fast. If stamping on the gas doesn't turn you on, I would show you right now what full speed means if I had it right here with me. It was a day like today, ready to start snowing, it rained but what a rain, it poured from the heavens. Mesogeion Avenue had turned into a lake when a call came to pick up a patient in Agia Paraskevi. Dispatch rated it as an urgent case, a man had fallen down and hit his head, it was serious. The paramedic guessed he had slipped in the rain.

I stamped on the gas. 'Watch out' yelled the other paramedic, 'You'll lose control and we'll crash.'

'Don't worry,' I assured him, 'I know what I'm doing,' and I gassed the ambulance even more in order to get to the patient on time."

"Do you really want us to believe you?" Stefanos cut him off savagely. "Tell the truth, this isn't how it happened. Forget the hot air you're sprouting to the idiots, I heard you one day when you were raving out of guilt. You were saying something different then."

"Am I the idiot?" asked Elvina.

"Anyway," the ambulance driver hung his head and broke down without answering the young girl directly, "I'll feel better if I get it off my chest. My conscience feels worse as long as I don't come clean or keep on changing the story."

"You have a conscience, let me laugh" said Stefanos ironically. It seems that he still had it in for Nontas since the time when the jerk had revealed his secrets.

Nowhere could a person find some quietness. Even here cries were heard, thought Elvina in between her trembling spells. I hoped I would find some tranquility here, but no such luck, she concluded, feeling really sad.

"I'll come clean," Nontas assured everyone. "I didn't start with the gas pedal pressed to the floor, I just sat behind the wheel, started the engine to warm up and the wipers to clear the turbid rain off the windscreen. I then looked at the two paramedics in my mirror and suggested that we go to a small taverna situated just down the road and have a bite, seeing that we had not eaten since dawn, and allow the bloody rain to stop, and then we could drive to pick up the injured person.

The guys didn't object so we parked on the pavement in front of the taverna and enjoyed the red wine and excellent appetizers. When we got back Dispatch was going wild, 'What happened, we lost you.'

'We had a flat tire and we're changing it,' the excuse was on the tip of my tongue, together with the taste of octopus casserole. What else can I say . . ." he stopped as if in shame and thus limited his words.

"What else can you say, that you finally picked up the man dead, that's what you forgot to say," Stefanos was both harsh and relentless.

"Yes," the former ambulance driver admitted shamefaced.

"How many times did you have a flat tire or some other problem, or was the delay in reaching the injured man quickly due to the red wine?"

"I don't know, it wasn't more than a few times," Nontas confessed with his head down, a real wreck.

"How many times? Say a number, an approximate number, as many as you can remember," Stefanos insisted relentlessly.

"Don't torment him anymore," pleaded the young girl.

"It may have been one more time, but there weren't many," the driver confessed vaguely but in a repentant tone. "I now understand that people lost their lives because of my negligence."

"Big deal, what do you need life for?" This gem came from the former cripple who had approached them after walking around the park and had uttered this one-liner without hearing what had been said before, just to join the conversation.

"I'm going to see what the children are doing. I don't want to hear anything else," the woman/mom—who had been a silent presence up to now—showed her indignation and quickly left.

Using the cripple's cleverness as his springboard, Nontas carried on:

"You're one hundred percent right, my friend. What do you need life for, especially a life likes yours, but my life isn't much better. You marry, have a family, kids, they all ignore you. Did you see any of them visiting me?"

"You've been dead for nearly two years now, Nontas. They threw you a funeral, memorial services, everything by the book. What else do you want?" Stefanos put him in his place.

"I'm not saying . . ." the short tallow-faced man took it all back, a man of short stature, a small man who just a minute ago had admitted that he was responsible for the death of a man. "But I'm not the only one," he expounded moralistically, "We're all champion loafers, and I don't want anyone saying anything to the contrary."

No one replied, and besides, the cripple didn't know what they were talking about. Stefanos went back into his shell again, but deeper than the glass pane isolating his photograph, while Elvina did not know whose side to take.

Nontas then seized her hand softly to attract her attention, as if seeking some solace.

"I had the most well-maintained vehicle in the fleet and I never crashed it once, no one can dispute that," the former ambulance-driver managed to emit a bitter laugh as he continued, "It'll soon be withdrawn from circulation," as a melancholic mask covered his face, eyes closed eyelashes singed. And not only his face, but also his neck and his body blackened with char that still gave off smoke, while the skin on his hands which had melted from the fire flowed thickly as a creamy mass, revealing the underlying bones.

"That's how they pulled me out of the accident on the highway," he explained to the young girl. "Who would have thought that I would be killed by a truck. Luckily I was in my own jalopy and so my ambulance was not damaged, nor did I kill the two paramedics." He was burning as he spoke and as he put a period to his words, all that remained was a puff of smoke and black ash on the ground that smelled of flesh.

"I wasn't the irresponsible person they said I was," as he tried to repair his image to Elvina, his burnt ash transforming back into a human form.

"Nontas, you're scaring me," she complained.

"Why my darling, do you also believe I was a bad person?" the former ambulance driver turned around, his sly restless eyes shining with tears.

"No, it's not that," she reassured him. How could she tell him that one moment she saw dead and the next as he was alive, or was this something that happened in the world of the dead. But he continued to plead his case:

"It was maybe once or twice that I didn't know what possessed me to go wild. I usually did more than my duty entailed. 'Grandpa,' I shouted as I got out of the vehicle to help my colleagues in transporting a helpless person. 'Grandpa, my name is Nontas and I will transport you to the hospital to get better. I gave him fortitude and that is the best medicine of all."

"It must have been when you had taken your shots, you had downed your tsipouro and you were in high spirits," Stefanos cut him off, doubting him.

"No, I wasn't drunk, one glass doesn't count." Nontas did not know what to say to defend himself but he did not give up. "I was the first to help load him into the ambulance. I passed through traffic-blocked Kiffisia Street as quick as you can say nutmeg. A mother who we were transporting together with her seriously injured child just could not believe it. 'My son would have died if it was not for you.' She looked me up to thank me but confessed that she still trembled thinking about the crazy ride . . ." He looked at all of them, sure that he had convinced them.

"Didn't you say that you liked travelling at high speed and that overtaking others turned you on?" It was the cripple who spoke out. "So that's why you speeded. It was not to help sick people."

"No, that's not true! I did my duty but my Department did not believe me when they asked me to tell my story. They decided that I was a danger to the Ambulance Services and suspended me. I would be appearing before the Board which would decide whether I should be dismissed or not. Who would have defended me when even all you guys are against me?" he cried out.

"How could I return home and tell my children what had happened to me after saying to them that they should grow up to be good and useful members of society. 'Okay Dad,' they replied to escape from me and then went on to do whatever they fancied.

Their mother conspired with them and the fucking thing was they were right, they didn't need me so I stopped interfering in their lives. From then on it was work and then the coffee-shop for tsipouro and backgammon. There was one two blocks away. It wasn't bad until the Department screwed me. How could I return home and tell them?

I jumped into my jalopy and drove around until I found myself on the highway without realizing it . . ."

"Where were you drinking that night? Stefanos intervened quietly.

"Somewhere, I stopped somewhere before joining the highway . . ." he had said a lot that was difficult to express. How could they continue to torment him, bent over the ground as he disappeared from Elvina's sight when she got up to walk away with Stefanos, away from the dead and their pathos.

"Where are we going?" she asked at some point as she didn't recognize where she was. It didn't look like Athens with its buses and apartment buildings. It was a road that encircled the harbor of an island. Its starting point touched the sea while the fishing caiques tied up against its mooring lines, reaching up to the regular service ship, and which at this moment was anchored in front of them. It was white and majestic with its high decks.

"Where are we? What's happening to us?" the young girl looked at Stefanos. From one moment to another they suddenly found themselves on an island, and they were surely on an island breathing in the yearly wind and the sea air

"I wanted to take you far away, so we could disappear for a while, I really needed it." Elvina wondered how they were transported but she dared not ask. A strong fear kept her from satisfying her curiosity which acted as if an adhesive tape covered her mouth, not allowing her to speak. She also knew that the answer would be much more painful than the sudden removal of the adhesive tape. Or perhaps nothing of that mentioned previously actually occurred and Stefanos and she had just disembarked from the regular service ship that was still disembarking passengers from its 'belly'. This could also have occurred since lately she was always getting lost. It was as if she had aberrations, could it have happened from the medications they had given her with the respirator, at the hospital where she had been treated.

But she overlooked it and besides, the positive aura and the radiance from the atmospheric affected her. She felt great so why should she be looking for something and be soul-searching?

"I had promised myself to come here with a girl, my girl . . . the woman I would love passionately so passionately that her absence would cause pain and deprivation. So in May I booked tickets and a room, I could pay for the trip. It wouldn't cost more than I had, such as a trip abroad, and as you may have gathered, I never did this when I was alive," Stefanos admitted as he continued his revelations.

"Mara, for whom I spoke to you about, was a real person but she never showed any interest in me. She was introduced to me in a bar, but this did not continue further. I never texted her to her cell-phone because I never knew her number. I asked for it but she avoided giving it to me. Everything I had inside me exploded when I saw her in the cosmetics store."

A melancholic cloud covered his face with his last words, but the air that was blowing moved it like a light veil and pushed it off him. The same wind also brought sea smells and salt to Elvina, pushing away all the old stories of Stefanos from her mind, allowing her to concentrate on the present events.

"The problem wasn't financial as I had enough money to pay for ten days on an island," said Stefanos, "so I started searching early as to which island I would take her to."

"Who?" asked Elvina as she saw a young couple out of the corner of her eye. They were young kids wearing jeans and backpacks as they laughingly competed as to who would first lick the chocolate ice cream ball on a cone.

"Imagine, they only bought one cone for the two of them," she interrupted Stefanos as she happily pointed them out to him. He continued his narration without answering her, while the veil that had been blown away by the wind was now permanently installed on his face.

"The girl and I never travelled to the island. I didn't come to the island with a girl because I never found one," he repeated. I leafed through all the travel guides and surfed the Internet, I chose Patmos as I was seduced by the view from the Monastery situated above the Hora. I then searched for my dream room, a studio next to the sea. It will be white, smelling of whitewash, cool because of the fresh cement floor that allows us to walk barefooted, so the coolness would rise from our soles and cover our whole body.

When it was midday we would go to the sea for hours on end. After drinking at the bars all night, we would then go for a swim in the dark under the moonlight. I missed nothing, I thought of everything, I forgot nothing. I booked the tickets, paid the deposit for the studio and then I waited for her, but she never came . . ." he stopped here, while the finely-spun veil that had installed itself on his face now transformed into a compact cover.

Elvina could only see a dark wall in place of his face and his characteristics, so she turned towards the island's quay. The young couple that was sharing a cone had meanwhile passed by them and had disappeared from sight.

"What happened next?" she asked as stories without a happy ending always turned her on and this story would surely not end happily.

"The woman for whom I had prepared the holidays and booked the room never appeared. I naturally did not go and I didn't bother canceling the tickets. And the following year I found myself here."

Elvina could not stop looking at the scenic view as Stefanos was speaking, nor did she look at him. The enchanting surroundings that included the island's quay, Apocalypse hill seen from above, caiques, boats and the regular service ship lying in the calm sky blue waters, all began to draw away, like a theatrical set moving to the sides to make way for the next set, which in Elvina's and Stefanos' case was the park, exactly there where they had been a little while ago, on Stefanos' bench in an open area where the gang congregated to talk.

"The enigma has been solved," Elvina told herself, "We didn't move at all. Transferring to the island was a suggestion or an illusion. It was a pity it finished so quickly," she sighed heavily.

"We should go again," offered Stefanos, who was resting his back on the wood, "The two of us should go again," he repeated to clarify the matter and Elvina raised no objection. As he turned around, his face took on a clean and serene look, with the eyes of the photograph looking at her adamantly, as if trying to hypnotize her.

"Elvina, don't you like me anymore?" she was brought back from the happy torpidity caused by Stefanos' penetrating stare by Nontas' complaining voice. The young man had disappeared. Where did he go? she thought and how much time did she lose without recanting what had taken place. Did she sleep, did she return home and to which home? This terrified her as Nontas continued:

"You're not talking to me, Elvina. Have I fallen irreparably in your eyes?"

"It's not that," replied the young girl and it wasn't a lie. "I was thinking of something . . ." she left her phrase incomplete which gave him the opening for a comeback. He kept moving, nervous and depressed, while his mouth remained open to utter sounds that would unburden him and possibly revive him.

"My family, my wife and children acted far worse than you. As soon as they had finished with the typical stuff, funerals and memorial services, they finished with me. They never visited me, leaving me all alone. 'He's finished and gone,' they wrote me off. Of course, they never took me seriously. I'd tell my daughter not to go somewhere but my wife would undermine me by saying she could go. 'You don't know,' she added later as she cut me out from the matter. They didn't think I could amount to something, and the last straw for them was when the Department dismissed me.

'The good-for-nothing really humiliated us with his goings-on,' they would say whenever they remembered me, which now would probably be almost never. I've gone to see them a couple of times after they had written me off, and you know what, the armchair I used to sit on to watch television had been pushed into a corner. Nothing else would verify that I used to live with them in the same house once upon a time," his bitterness made him stop talking.

"Relax, you're making it into a tragedy," Elvina tried to placate him.

"I've degenerated down to the same level as this poor sod," cried Nontas without tears, pointing to whom he meant. "That punk over there," he said, and as soon as the conversation moved on, moving from him to someone else, he again found his cool.

Elvina turned to see who he was pointing to and noticed a shabby man of around forty who was running behind the tufts of the trees, holding in his hands small bags filled with koliva, that is boiled wheat offered at memorial services, two or three bags in each palm.

"He lives on koliva and little rusks served at the refectory after a funeral," Nontas said cheerfully, filling in the details while reverting back to his old self again.

"He lives in a small shack next to the wall. The keepers let him wander around the park. He sometimes stands at the gate begging for money or helps to park the cars for a tip, while other times he sits in the refectory drinking coffee, hoping to grab a small bottle of brandy from the tables, as well as all the koliva that have remained. "That's how he lives," he chuckled, "Koliva is good for you, wheat, sugar and raisins, nutritious food. You see, he is alive and needs to eat and drink."

The chuckling now turned into jeering as a bell suddenly peeled out insistently and excruciatingly in Elvina' mind. Really, when had she last eaten? But where had Nontas suddenly disappeared to, leaving her all alone?

Her eyes flickered from tree to tree but she just could not flush out the short active man. Further down, a group of people were walking from the church, dressed in black as if they had attended a memorial service. The man who lived on koliva followed about ten meters behind them, hoping to secure today's rations. Elvina approached him, hoping to talk to him.

"Forget them, come and eat with me," she suggested. Close-by he wasn't so bad-looking if you ignored his grubbiness and the unkempt beard growing on his cheeks.

He ignored her completely so Elvina nudged him to draw his attention.

"I'm talking to you," she was now pissed off as she stood a meter away from him. Very few or probably no man would remain indifferent to her tall slender body, her sweet face and her bountiful hair.

He however did not budge an eyelid, nor did he give any indications that a girl—ugly or pretty—was standing right next to him. He could touch her if he raised his hand.

She shivered as this was not normal. Something was wrong with her or with him; it was probably her. She approached the group of people who were leaving the church and walking uphill towards the grave, holding the tray with the bags of koliva . . . koliva with her name printed on the bags.

At the same time the park suddenly filled up with church monuments that were graves: small, large, family plots, candles sitting on the marble slabs. She looked left and right, frightened as she milled around, but the change was general and absolute, terminative. Trees shaded the monuments, endless rows of graves separated by small narrow pathways—a real labyrinth. What she saw as monuments were in fact large family graves. There were no lights, only lit candles on marble slabs whose illuminations barely showed the slab with the cross on it. Just a few benches remained for the relatives and visitors of the dead.

She was in a cemetery. She looked left and right to make sure, there was no doubt. The cool park was nothing more than a cemetery with tall trees and thick vegetation, including bushes and shrubs, flowerbeds and vases with flowers that adorned the church monuments; it was a typical cemetery from one end to the other.

She self-consciously found herself at the front of the procession that zigzagged between the graves as it proceeded for the memorial service, with the tray holding the koliva leading the way. It was true, the koliva did have her name. Her name, "ELVINA", was traced out in long, thin, silver beadlike sugared almonds on icing sugar that covered the koliva.

The koliva were for her; awareness came as a thunderbolt and was completely irreversible. The tray was accompanied by her mother and father, her mother dressed in black and sobbing, her father wearing a black tie and black armband, his countenance serious and silent.

"They buried her in Athens because she liked it there, as she never returned to the island." She heard these spoken words as if they were emanating from a tunnel. The voice was that of a distant relative whom Elvina had never met and who lived in Athens, speaking to probably his wife.

"So they won't be visiting her very often," concluded the unknown person, expressing these words with the right amount of sadness that was proper for this memorial service.

"This was the first time that they could come since the funeral. Her mother was sick caused by her grief. It's a shame they lost their little girl," responded her aunt, who lived on the island but had come to the service to be with the parents. Amongst the last was Kostas, thoughtful, closed in the shell of his face.

Elvina passed by him as Natalia, her friend from school, walked faster to hug her mother. Elvina watched as they both cried. Other relatives and some acquaintances followed behind her mother and friend, when they stopped in front of a grave. Her mother fell onto the marble slab and hugged it as she sobbed pitifully, her sobbing passing through the tunnel so that Elvina could hear it loud and clear and even Elvina was shaken emotionally.

She managed to pass her relatives with difficulty in order to reach the grave. She had to be certain, she had to see if the grave was hers or not, even if it devastated her.

She stood between her parents and looked at the grave. It was an austere marble slab and a cross. Her name was inscribed on the cross, together with the dates of birth and death.

Elvina felt her skin tearing from the sudden ice-cold flash of awareness . . . she was dead. Thoughts arose from the depths of her mind. Why didn't they stay on the island, what made them come to Athens so she would see them. Their presence, the koliva and the service killed Elvina.

"Everyone passes through a transitional phase," Stefanos was standing next to her, wearing the plastic face of the photograph as a mask. "We all pass through the phase of not knowing what has happened until we accept the fact that we are dead."

Elvina was still unable to accept what had happened to her, not that she had not suspected it, otherwise why was she always in the park.

Her mother was now covering the marble slab with rose-petals. The grave was covered in flowers.

"So that's why they bring flowers," she told Stefanos, "If you cut the flowers, they die and that's why they bring them to funerals. They're dead just like us."

Stefanos did not reply but he was there for her.

After the flowers, her friend and her father held her mother as they returned back to mundane earthy matters, passing by the refectory. The others followed, leaving Elvina and Stefanos alone at the grave. She bent over to touch the petals that were still warm from the hands of her mother. The warmth touching her cold skin was like a lightning bolt. Yes, she was cold and dead and this awareness shattered her.

"You're number 33Δ," Nontas informed her, shouting next to her since Elvina felt as if she was in the depths of the earth, covered with soil, as if an earthquake had occurred and she was buried in the ruins. "Your grave is near that of Stefanos, two rows to the left," the ambulance driver continued on loquaciously.

Elvina stood up and brushed the soil from her body, together with her mother's rose-petals.

She suddenly realized that she had killed herself. One night she was in the apartment she had moved into with Sonia and was burning with a high fever and a terrible cough, as well as dyspnea. She was wheezing heavily. Her room-mate, frightened, offered to take her to the hospital.

"No!" I was adamant, "I know what to take, antibiotics and cortisone sprayed into my nose. I have some in my cupboard from the last time."

She wouldn't let me get up, she brought the medicines herself with a glass of water. I swallowed two pills together and inhaled umpteen doses of cortisone to treat my respiratory system. I woke up good as new the next day.

"See, it wasn't serious," I crowed, but how long did this recovery last? It was about a week later that I was taken to the hospital. I seem to hear Sonia's voice called for an ambulance as I floated weightlessly in the wind, babbling deliriously from the high fever.

I can hardly remember my stay in the hospital. Did I die and was somewhere else; the thought that this was the end never entered my mind.

I was lying in bed filled with various machines and instruments, serums attached to my arms as they dripped nutritional liquids into my body, but it was too late. I might have saved myself if I had gone earlier for treatment. Why didn't I do it?

Anger frothed out of her mouth, mixing with the soil from the grave and gluing to her body and clothes, turning into mud. Tears accompanied the froth, running from her eyes, turning the soil on her face into a layer of mud, a shell that she tried to break through grimaces but could not shatter it.

She realized that she was beginning to resemble Stefanos, like his motionless face. I'll stand up and remove the mud. I'll wash myself at the tap and clean my dress.

How come I did not understand before the dress that I was buried in, that's why I didn't have any other clothes. Let me get up now, she told herself. What's happened has happened, everything has finished now. I am number 33Δ, why do I complain about?

"We have numbers here my girl," Nontas explained now what he had hidden from her previously, when she had not known then. "We have numbers here my girl, which the relatives look for, together with the names. They would never find us otherwise. Section A, row 3 grave 23, that's me," and he burst out laughing. "Try and understand with names only, people don't die alphabetically."

"I'm 33Δ," she repeated so she would remember it.

"You're a doll," Nontas' voice was heard next to her.

"Nontas, you're really bugging me. Can't you see how disheveled I look? I'm covered in mud and soil, how can I be a doll?"

"You look great!" the short little man smiled at her.

Elvina then looked down at herself. Her body was as always firm and slender, her dress like new, the silk shining in the sun. Her long hair caressed her back and the mirror that was the glass pane covering Stefanos' photograph showed her face clean and soft. When she raised her arm to touch her face it was cold, but she would get used to it.

It began at the funeral. Who was being buried? Elvina just could not remember. It was as if a cloudy mist covered her memory. It was someone she knew, possibly a relative or a friend. In any event, she went to the funeral. As she returned from the grave she was looking at the headstones. Quite a few had photographs on them. This was common practice, especially if the deceased was a young person. She stopped at the grave of a young man. His face couldn't have been more than thirty. A sweet young man who gazed at her behind the glass pane.

"He must have been sick to have died so young," she thought immediately. "No he wasn't sick," this second thought cancelling out the first, but it wasn't a thought, it was Stefanos talking to her and the funeral was her own.

It was my funeral and as I passed by Stefanos' grave, he spoke to me and I heard him. If I wasn't dead I would not have heard him. And when I went to the sports shop to buy the ball for the small bald-headed boy, no one paid any attention to me because I was dead. And many more inexplicable things happened to me because no one could see me. The dead can see the dead and the living can see the living.

There are some exceptions of course, such as the little girl who could see Stefanos and her swimming in the sea while her mother could not, and she even scolded her daughter for it.

"Let's go to the seaside to find the little girl who can see us," she asked Stefanos, in a desperate attempt to keep in touch with a living soul. Surely he would indulge her.

"Leave the little one in peace, you shouldn't do it," Nontas stopped them, his gaunt body acting as a shield. Realizing that he was right, Elvina backed down.

"How can we search a whole beach, and it's not summer so why should she go to the beach?" She expressed various reasons not to go, so all that was left was for her to look harassed and troubled at the trees that hid only church monuments and crosses, without finding a way to escape.

An unknown form then appeared, brushing off leaves as it spoke in a deep voice which, after passing through layers of earth and exiting the surface, then resembled a blocked up loudspeaker.

"I've been here awhile but have never come out, but for you I'll make an exception. You're the most ethereal person that has ever come here. I'll take you wherever you want to go" and it reached out a pair of arms as it was uttering phonemes.

Elvina moved back in fright as the horrible illusion approached her, lowering itself to her level. It was nothing more than a clutter of worn-out bones tied loosely together. This could have resulted from trying to talk through its ancient jaws that for years have remained motionless, causing the ligaments to atrophy and the bones to grind against each other, a sound that terrified the young girl. She tried to escape the moving scarecrow, falling down onto the ground to hide. But she would not let the ground hide her so she stood up covered in dust and ran away.

Behind her, Stefanos, together with Nontas and the cripple, prevented the skeleton from chasing her. As soon as Stefanos learnt that Elvina had surpassed the stage between the living and the dead and was now theirs, he now wanted to be near her. The three men crashed into it, smashing its bones to pieces, while the skeleton just barely managed to collect the pieces to put them back into its grave. By that time Elvina had stopped at a tap on the other side of the cemetery to drink some water and to catch a few breaths, trying to recover from the fright she had received.

She drank some water and recovered somewhat.

"Water rejuvenates me," Marilena Evangelou, the famous actress had said when the two of them were reflected in the shiny water surface as it flowed in the stream to nowhere. "It keeps me strong," maintained the Theatrical Diva, who used any means available—including Elvina—to win over a love that she never acquired when she was alive, and which she never ever managed to achieve.

Elvina felt the desperation of Marilena Evangelou deep in her bosom, which resembled her own, having died so young before managing to love and be loved. So mimicking the majestic actions of the actress with respect to the waters that never stopped flowing, she spread out her legs into the crystallized clear waters to draw in its energy.

Elvina then scooped up some water in her cupped hands to clean her cheeks and forehead, and to clear her head from the dizziness and giddiness resulting from the knowledge that she was dead. The young girl then wetted her hair under the tap, the water running down to the lacy hemline of her dress. She never had so much hair in her life. She brought it in front of her to cover her breasts. She looked like a fairy as she took the stance of an unworldly incorporeal form, allowing her hair to draw her away. Her hair fluttered in the wind, carrying her up to the pavilion . . . the pavilion with its rich greenery where they hung out in the old times when she believed she was still alive. They took her to the pavilion which they visited often and which became her haven with Stefanos.

There were no crosses and marble slabs in the pavilion as far as she could see in between the creepers and the twilight.

"Tell me really what this is," Elvina asked Stefanos who had come with her.

"An old family grave. It hasn't been used for years. They don't bury anyone here so no living person comes here," the man next to her explained quietly.

"It doesn't look like a grave," whispered the young girl.

"It looks like a little house in a garden, as I had told you," Stefanos finished her phrase. "Eleonora and Nikos, the couple who had erected it, were somewhat eccentric. They asked to be buried in their house and since this was impossible, they brought a piece of their garden here."

"This is the grave of Eleonora and Nikos?" she shivered as she said this.

"The two of them loved each other very much," Stefanos explained, "They were together for over fifty years. When he passed away, she soon followed him."

The pavilion was now unrecognizable. The garlands made out of supple creeper stalks with green leaves that dripped freshness which had adorned the construction were now dry and withered. They were barely holding on to the rails. Eleonora never came out of her grave after the notorious and decisive show, nor did Nikos. So they withdrew forever, leaving the pavilion to wither away. When Elvina went in, she noticed a piece of pale, weak grass trying to grow but as it was now not watered, it was just managing to survive.

"Eleonora has left her pad, she doesn't need it anymore," Stefanos whispered behind her. Elvina then cracked a small bitter smile as a thought flashed through her mind that she was beginning to resemble Stefanos, but could they love each other as they were now both dead? They were both the same.

We died before we could love and be loved, can we perhaps find love after death? She kept her bitter smile on her lips as she turned towards the young man.

"I will look after the pavilion. I can manage it. At home I cared for huge pot plants with living green plants, it was a small but wonderful garden. I'll liven up the pavilion so we can both stay here. I'll care for the greenery, I'll plant more flowers, it'll be more beautiful than before," she allowed a smile to appear on her face.

"I never went to Prague," confided Stefanos, "Nor did I go with another woman. I only went with you and that's the only recollection I have. I remember having you next to me in the bar with the opaque colored glass in the windows and the husky music that transformed everything into a vision."

Elvina's only response was to look at him and sweeten the smile that was permanently on her lips, an expression that suggested the two of them might work things out between them.

They left behind them the pavilion that had rejuvenated them and began to walk along the pathway. Relaxed and remote, each with his thoughts but also with new thoughts born from love, while innumerable light shadows watched them from behind the trees, floating just above the ground. Some were invisible due to their age while other more recent ones were clearly visible. Some were unknown and inaccessible while others were more familiar, such as Nontas who was snickering slyly, the cripple who was testing the flexibility of his limbs, the drunkard who had raised his hand as if holding a glass of wine, the woman/mom who was busy choosing balls, the journalist who had raised his camera, as well as some less familiar ones.

They were all happy with the love-story that had suddenly blossomed among the headstones as the sun shining over the cemetery turned into twilight. A twilight that gradually folded the colors of the day, pushing them into the depths of the horizon, until the light from the lit candles illuminated the dense texture of the shadows that came and went into the darkness.

End